WOTHWOOD
A BROKEN CITIES NOVELLA

WOTHWOOD
A BROKEN CITIES NOVELLA

Natania Barron

Falstaff Books
Charlotte, North Carolina

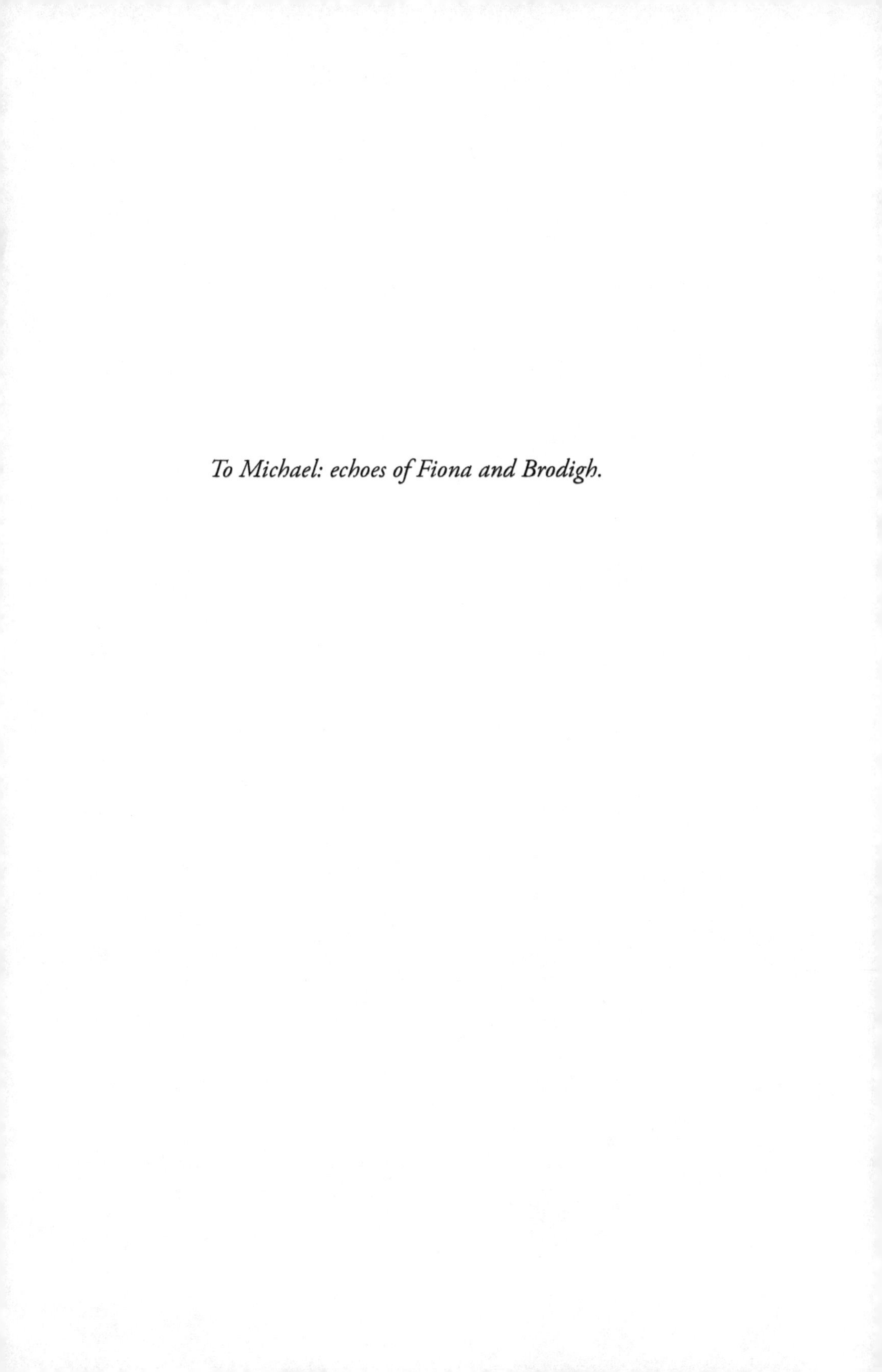

To Michael: echoes of Fiona and Brodigh.

Tho' much is taken, much abides; and tho'
We are not now that strength which in old days
Moved earth and heaven, that which we are, we are;
One equal temper of heroic hearts,
Made weak by time and fate, but strong in will
To strive, to seek, to find, and not to yield.

- Alfred, Lord Tennyson

PROLOGUE

BRAIG VANN.

That was his name.

What a good lad. What a big lad. Going to be the mormaer, for sure, when his father dies.

Like a warlord of old, back when Brezhia wasn't beholden…

All his life it was his name.

Big as a tree and twice as strong. You'll be a warrior, son. You'll put them all to shame.

Except now it wasn't.

Didn't matter much since he was going to bleed out all over the ground, anyway. He may have been the strongest, biggest of the brood back at home in Bannercliffe, but out here in the Wothwood, he was flesh and blood and nothing more.

The mormaer is dead, long live the heir. Braig Vann!

Kill a pig, bleed him good. Bleed him clean and make good sausages.

His whole body was sticky with the blood. And it looked like he'd wet his pants from it. Like some terrified little child. Except it wasn't piss, it was his life. What was left of it.

Served him right, he supposed. Goddess Noduuoret would never forgive him. No one entered the Wothwood and came out alive. No one. But he hadn't taken the warnings seriously enough, and when he saw the boar in the distance, he broke from the hunting party and selfishly tried to make the kill alone. He wanted to make a name for himself: Braig Vann, Boar Killer.

No more.

Braig Vann. His father's name, his mother's eyes. That was his name.

Except he'd lost it, now.

How did that happen?

Oh, yes.

Because Glannon showed up in the Wothwood. A few moments before, a lifetime ago. It was getting hard to remember when he was dying so fast.

But who was she? His mother? Grandmother? His mind skipped like a stone across a creek. No, cousin. Cousin Glannon Bel. She showed up, merry cheeks flushed with exertion and excitement at the chase, her wild hair down about her shoulders. How many times had he thought of drawing his hands through those tousled brown locks? How many nights had he awoken, thinking of her? Too many and not enough.

And now she appeared to him, venturing deeper into the Wothwood than she should have, to save him. To help him. To bring him succor in his time of need. Because that was the only explanation.

For a dizzy moment, he thought he was living in a story of old come to life.

But then she said, "I'm sorry."

Braig wanted to tell her how beautiful she was. How much he envied her. How every time they sparred, he was really thinking of kissing her and smothering her. That she would have made a better mormaer than he, and it wasn't fair that he had a better claim because he was a man. She had the better qualifications.

But nothing came from his lips except a wet moan.

There were no tears on her face, now. Not like when she had stood by him and wept, just earlier that day, as they mourned his father, Marchan Vann, greeting the morning rays of the sun. The hunt was in honor of him, wasn't it?

The details of his life slurred together alarmingly, but his body was too tired to fight it.

She didn't say anything, just watched him.

Everything was so quiet. And getting quieter. The ringing in his ears faded to a dull roar, and now Braig struggled against the dimming of everything.

Why wouldn't she help him?

With what could only be described as a monumental effort, he lifted his hand toward her, upwards as if in appeal to the goddess herself.

"Braig," said Glannon Bel, and he couldn't tell where her voice was coming from. "I'm sorry, but I have to let you die."

Let him die? Braig wanted to protest, but he found his voice was gone. It had once been so easy to use, but now…

"Now that your father's dead, and my mother's dead, I'm free of my debt. I can share what I've always known. That you're not of us. You're not of Bannercliffe," she said, taking a deep breath. She let it out slowly and continued, as if she'd rehearsed this bit many times over. "Your mother, rest her soul, was raped by

Therian soldiers and guilted your father into raising you as his own. My mother knew, and she passed the death oath to me. And now I pass it to you. Because you know you can't inherit your father's seat, now, and that leaves me."

Glannon had the loveliest voice. Rough in the right places. Like wind through rye. A sighing, whispery quality to it. It was one of Braig's favorite things. But why was it forming such horrible words?

In his delirious state, he thought her lips were turning to black feathers, whirling about in the wind as they were formed, sounded, and reduced back to silence. Had Glannon Bel always spoken in feathers?

Braig let the words assemble in his mind, but the wood felt like it was breathing at him, and he gave up.

"So, the stories tell me that I've got two choices. I can kill you with my own hand—though the boar's done a good job of that so far—or I can leave you to fate," said the feathers. The words. Glannon.

Braig tried to say something, but he just made a wet sound. He hated how weak his body was all of a sudden. The one thing he had relied on for near twenty years was failing him marvelously.

Such a big lad, such a strong lad. A warrior of old.

Glannon wiped her hands on her thighs, feathers falling all around her, but she didn't seem to notice. They were white now, tipped in blue. "You know how I am. I believe that fate makes the way for us. The beast found you, and the Wothwood claimed you. That's how the story will go."

"Glaaaaan…" It was as close as Braig could say.

She was leaving, walking away. Swallowed up in a thousand shimmering wings.

"Fate, Braig. It's just fate," she said. "Fate that drew my mother to the Wothwood to die; fate that ate your father from the inside out. Fate that called you here. I can't be blamed for that. And I really am sorry."

At least he got to see her backside one last time before he died. Even if he had no name and no purpose and was returning back to the ground along with the boar he'd killed.

But not even that lasted. The last thing Braig saw was leaves passing over his eyes.

There was a man at his crotch.

This was the first of a few startling realizations on Braig's part. If he'd had much strength at all, the sort he usually had, he'd have taken the bastard and bashed his brains against the nearest tree. But as things stood, it felt as if someone had removed all his muscles and replaced the sinew with water and twigs. And none of them intersected, either. Somehow everything was heavier than it should be. Was the rest of him sand? Or was he tied down?

It was dark, not long before twilight, and Braig couldn't help but shake the dim regret of having not died. Because being alive meant he was shamed by Glannon Bel. It meant that he was left for dead. And, with this unfamiliar person poking about his nethers, clearly none of his people had even come looking for them.

Bannercliffe. He should, by all rights, be the one parading into the village with the boar, drunk on the sweet ambrosia of battle. But he was…

A shot of pain burned down the inside of his thigh.

And then came a voice. A bit high, almost squeaky.

"You shouldn't be out here in the Wothwood."

Braig could say nothing, but he used the energy left to him to keep his eyes open. He rolled them in response.

"Brezhians. Never fucking know where to tread to keep away the beasties," said the man.

Braig rolled his eyes again.

"If I decide to fix you, you'll owe me."

His would-be savior came into view. Garish bright clothes. Covered in buttons. A huge hat that would look ridiculous one the most ostentatious Yerevan whore.

A tyckner.

Braig's head swam. What were tyckners doing out in the Wothwood? He felt sick.

"Or, I could let you die. Like that buxom lass just did," the tyckner said, resting back on his heels. "Interesting family you have, sounds like. I've always found you folks terribly difficult to understand."

It was getting dark, but Braig honestly couldn't tell if that was from the blood loss or the darkening of the Wothwood.

Had Glannon Bel really left him to die?

Though given the sheer amount of pain right now, dying might not be so bad.

"But then," said the tyckner, "you couldn't exact revenge if you died. You couldn't remake yourself." He paused a moment for drama. "This is a universal language, as different as we may be. Lords and ladies of the firmament, but you've lost a tremendous quantity of blood."

Braig still didn't give an answer.

"I don't think you've much time, in my expert opinion," said the tyckner, clicking his tongue. "Have you made peace with your goddess? Noduuoret, that's her name, right? This here being her burial ground and all."

Braig found that, though he never considered himself a praying man, or a traditionalist in terms of religion, knowing he was a few breaths from death imbued him with rather impressive amount of zealotry.

"Help me, then," Braig said, the words taking so much effort to say he could taste new blood in his throat. "By the goddess's city, I swear…"

"Ah, well, yes, that's the right idea," said the man. "I *will* need something in return."

"I'll… pay my debt… to you."

"Ten years," said the tyckner, no hesitation. As if he'd rehearsed the line a thousand times. "And ten bodies. You live as my bodyguard. Help me in my business, learn the way of the tyckners. And then, if we have time, we'll figure out this mess of yours, Braig Not-Vann."

Braig nodded. His lips were numb, and words were hard to form. But he was able to ask the man's name.

"Poole," said the tyckner. "Sid Poole." One bright moment later, Braig's world faded from view as Poole tightened the tourniquet around his thigh and went to work.

CHAPTER ONE
PROFESSOR

PROFESSOR AODA KANNA WAS TIRED OF BEING MISTAKEN FOR A WHORE. As part of the Therian company assembled for the purpose of establishing the first settlement inside the borders of the Wothwood, the endless forest in the Brezhian territory, she had been selected for her keen intelligence, general knowhow, and excellent survival skills. She had not one, but three, university degrees: history, geology, and practical physics. But as she was the lone woman among a throng of men, the assumption of her occupation persisted, regardless of what little village they came across during the trek south. From Muline to West Coru, it was always the same.

It wouldn't have been so bad save that the assumption was continually showered with adjectives and commentary. It was always the *ugly* whore. Or the *well-used* whore. Or the *deformed* whore.

It was hardest to be reminded of her physical deformities day in and day out. In all truth, being called a whore was no concern to her. Her mother was a whore, after all.

Her mother, Koleta, was a remarkable woman with many talents besides whoring. Not that it mattered. Still, it was whoring that got Aoda a good education, and it was whoring that put food on the table. She should be grateful. Thankful, even, to have been given such an opportunity.

Still, her ears went red when people thought it was her trade. And it did nothing to make her curdled milk countenance any brighter or more attractive. The only way most of the people they came across—even though they were, technically, her people, by a half at least—could imagine a woman in such a position as her was if she was under a man. Quite literally.

"Surely you could have afforded… a more, um… less wretched whore," a big Brezhian by the name of Bozal said, clicking his tongue at Aoda. Bearded. Burly. The picture of Brezhian masculinity.

Wretched. That was a new one.

Never let a person decide your worth by your appearance, her mother had told her on countless occasions. Except that was literally her mother's line of work.

Everything was based on what she looked like. And though Aoda knew her mother meant well by the sentiment, hoping that her daughter's life would be judged on her merit and not her disfigurement, it was never an option.

"She's our *surveyor*," corrected Captain Adamen Moll. He was always quick to clarify but far from gallant about it. The captain had been insulted when she'd been assigned to this regiment, having written a formal petition of complaint to Lord Re himself. But Captain Moll had asked for the most intelligent surveyor in the university system, and that's precisely what he got. "And she's damned good at her job. Even if she isn't pleasing to look upon."

That was as close to a compliment as she'd get from the handsome Therian. He, bronze and fit, his black hair always trimmed and oiled, his face clean-shaven, his teeth straight. Captain Moll had the look of a man who was planned. Whose parents saw in themselves a more perfect expression of beauty and coupled for the mere reason of his conception and eventual existence. An artist could no better have carved him into black marble.

Aoda, as it was, found him impossibly handsome and charming, even knowing their chances of romance were less likely than a chicken being birthed by a horse. She was stocky and pock-marked and half blind in one eye. But even Captain Moll couldn't argue she knew what she as doing, and had proven useful on a dozen different occasions. If being intelligent and helpful got her noticed, she'd make that her number one priority while traveling with his regiment.

"Oh, of course," the big Brezhian said. He was scratching his curly beard, his fingers vanishing every few moments and then reappearing like white maggots, their ends dirty and peeling.

Aoda winced. It was hard to believe her mother was descended from these barbaric people.

"No offense meant," added the Brezhian.

"None taken, of course," added Lieutenant Ori Shenbar, Moll's right hand man and true diplomat of the surveying party. If there was anyone who Aoda could consider a friend, he was closest to that.

Shenbar was a cousin of Moll's, broad and well-built, but with the heart of a poet. He was the silvered voice of reason, and Aoda had heard he was on the fast track to be appointed as an ambassador to one of the newly acquired Kargr territories to the north. As such, this was to be his last tour with Moll.

Some men would have used that time to drink and whore as much as possible, and though those were always two viable options where the regiment traveled, Shenbar wasn't about it. He was focused on his work—sometimes so much so that it made him boring to be around—and that was admirable.

"None taken, of course," Captain Moll said, slapping Aoda on the back hard enough to make her cough. "Well, our surveyor's unfortunate countenance has proved a point of confusion now and again, so you are not the first to make such an assumption. But she doesn't let that get to her, does she?"

Shenbar intoned, clearing his throat, "Of course she doesn't. Professor Kanna, and indeed our entire regiment, is infused with the tenacity of Theria. Valiant. Strong. Focused on the betterment of the Empire, by virtue of his Lord Re."

"Brezhian?" asked Bozal, staring again at Aoda, ignoring ninety percent of what Shenbar had said. "Kanna's a Brezhian name."

"My mother is an expatriate," explained Aoda, correcting herself midway. "I grew up in the grand city of Yereva. But I'm a bastard, I'm afraid, and no knowledge of my patrilineal inheritance. Still, for all intents and purposes, I consider myself a Therian."

The Brezhian spat on the ground. "And you sound like one, don't you? Amazing what a lifetime away from the trees will do to a person. Who'd your mother fight for, then? Imagine she fell on the side of Chief Koulm. Most of the Kannas ended up that side of things, too ashamed to show their faces this side of the Blue River."

Aoda honestly didn't know. Her mother never spoke of her time living in Brezhia, nor of her people. Altough Aoda's accent was the rounded vowels of Yereva and Thalia, her mother Koleta, had maintained the harsher tones of Brezhia all her life. Her identity, though, was a continual mystery. And whenever Aoda asked her mother of her life before arriving in Yereva as a young girl, it seemed an impenetrable wall was put up behind them.

Some children might have pressed for more details, but Aoda was different. She knew her deformities caused her mother a great deal of guilt. Like many children of brothel, she carried the scars of disease often associated with the trade. Unlike many others, she herself did not carry the disease, though her body was forever scarred. Her ugly, twisted teeth, her rheumy eyes, her stunted height. Growing up in the brothel, she had seen children worse off than she:

little horrors with holes for faces, hands like claws, missing noses... She knew she had escaped a more terrible fate.

Still, Aoda, grew up with a "risen soul" as her mother would say. She always knew her mother's mood and never wanted to contribute to her suffering. Especially as she became older and less in demand, weaving sorrow around herself like a bower. It was Aoda's work that paid for Koleta's small apartment in Yereva and kept food on the table when her mother could not be bothered to get out of bed.

But this trip was not purely for profit. This assignment dovetailed perfectly with her own work, namely research regarding the Great Vanishment, which she had spent the better part of the last decade studying along with her mentor, Professor Suen, back at the Collegia of Yereva. They were working to explain how, two thousand years ago, most of the metals in Theria, Brezhia, and beyond vanished. In one cataclysmic moment—reported as a star falling to the earth by the Therians and as a goddess thrusting an ancient sword into the Wothwood by the Brezhians—most metal vanished. Gone from active mines and rich lodes.

Anything metal within the composition of the earth itself had been pulled elsewhere with a kind of magnetic event, especially copper and iron. Therian glass replaced metal in some cases, in arrowheads and spears, but few new metal devices could be made again. And given the degradation of the metals, every passing year, fewer could be made. In some cases, families had reforged swords over a hundred times.

She had spent the better part of her academic life tracing, collecting geologic data and stories, and slowly finding herself led back to Brezhia, her mother's land, for answers. And, specifically, to the Wothwood itself. That damned, forbidden place. But forbidden why? She was quite certain it was because it held an unfathomable fortune of metal. Copper and iron to be sure, but more besides. Like silver. Like gold. So precious that its value could not be measured. When the emperor heard of her work, and its promise, he had sent his best. Or at least, what he could afford to gamble when it came to the Brezhians. Their peace was already strained, and they were extremely protective of the Wothwood, even if they never ventured in it themselves.

"The Professor is beholden to Yereva only, I assure you. A Therian heart beats true," Shenbar said.

"The Professor is beholden to the pursuit of knowledge," Aoda corrected. "And the Therian cause."

Bozal looked disgusted. "Well, you're not in Yereva today. And you need Bozal's help." He punched his chest making a sickening hollow sound.

"That is why we sought you out," said Shenbar, the exasperation slipping through his voice ever so slightly. "We were told that Bozal the Bold is an expert on the Grave of Noduuoret."

At this, Bozal straightened slightly. Aoda noticed that the endless beard pulling came to an abrupt stop.

"Did you hear that, now?" he asked at length.

"Yes. And now that Brezhia and Theria are united under the banner of the Lord Re, we have been sent out as emissaries into the Wothwood to set up a fortification, the first of its kind, to begin the necessary expansion of our lands," said Shenbar, reaching for the long proclamation he carried with him at all times, the one signed by the Lord Re himself. "It would likely not serve as—"

"No."

Bozal's proclamation took everyone by surprise, especially Captain Moll, who blanched and then narrowed his eyes. Aoda thought he might strike the man, but he didn't. She'd seen him more violent over lesser offenses.

"But there's your ancestral home to consider," Shenbar pressed. "The lost city of the goddess."

This did not help matters more even in the slightest.

"I said no," Bozal said. "And the city's a myth, stranger. You're just as likely to find Noduuoret's city as you are to find a prick on a mare."

Then Captain Moll asked, "Your pardon?" *No* was not a word he was accustomed to hearing, especially in such vulgar terms.

"No, I won't be fucking guiding you or telling you or giving you anything related to Noduuoret's Grave or the fucking Wothwood," Bozal pressed, taking a step back from the small circle they'd created outside of his village, peppering his phrase with as much profanity as possible. "Goddess's piss, did I stutter?"

"That seems quite final," Shenbar said, trying one last time. Aoda admired his pluck, even if it was sadly misplaced. "There's coin in it for you. Plenty of it. Your children look half starved."

"They'll make do. We've lived on the borders of Wothwood since before our people had a name. And we might not live in grand palaces or send our children to Godshit Universities," Bozal said, his eyes narrowing at Aoda. "But we're fine the way it is."

"But there hasn't been a party to Noduuoret's Grave in nigh on ten years," Shenbar said. "You're hiding from an invisible threat. Our surveyors and historians account for an amazing wealth of resources just beyond your grasp. As proud members of the Empire…"

"No," Bozal roared. "I said fucking no!"

When Captain Moll made to strike the Brezhian, Shenbar was quick to jump between them.

"Is there anyone else you're familiar with who might be willing to give us some information on the subject?" the lieutenant asked sweetly, in spite of having to struggle to keep his captain from doing yet another regretful act. "Another clan, perhaps?"

"I could have you tried for treason, you know," hissed Captain Moll, "This is *Theria* now, you ingrate."

Bozal's face flushed, arms up in preparation to fight. For a moment, Aoda was certain they were going to see blood. He lowered his fists, though, thinking better, and wiped at his mouth. "Try the tyckners. There's a caravan not far from here, squatting on our land as usual. One of 'em called Poole something, he might be willing to sell his soul."

"You know we have every capability of getting the information we want from you," Captain Moll said, breathing hard and brushing off the front of his doublet. "If we don't find what we need, we'll be back."

Aoda cleared her throat, hoping to distract even if just a small amount. Big men ever did have the habit of raising each other's hackles. And by the looks of Bozal, he wouldn't go down without a fight. "If we're to make for the tyckners, we'll have to leave soon. Only an hour or so before sunset, sir."

"I know damned well what time it is, Kanna," spat the captain, turning on his heel and shouting to the regiment to begin moving on.

Chapter Two
Mormaer

GLANNON **B**EL WAS TIRED OF WEARING THE MORMAER'S DIADEM. **I**T pressed against her temples, weighed down the crown of her head, growing heavier every year for the last seven. She remembered how much she wanted it, as a young girl, when her uncle Marchan was mormaer. It was an object of desire, a symbol of great power. Each section forged from a different metal, links and chains cascading down the back in an array of colors and designs; bits of money forged into the jeweled circlet and in the long chains and additions made to it over the years. Those broken, repaired. Motley and lovely and so very precious.

They even had a single blacksmith assigned to its upkeep. Per Madoc, her most trusted advisor, as well. Only they were allowed to hold the diadem.

She was allergic to one of the silvery sections, though, and had to always be careful not to put it on her skin. Yet somehow, it always found its way there. And as she listened to yet another petitioner from town, Uuan again, complain about the missing yoke from his homestead, she could feel the itching sensation rise and grow and burn at her neck. She wanted to scratch it, to dig her nails into the flesh and burst the inevitable boil rising in response.

But instead of scratching in an uncomely manner, Glannon Bel willed her face still, her eyes open, and kept perfectly straight in the flat-bottomed Chair of Rule.

Being a mormaer is all about poise, she recalled her mother telling her once. *Never let them see your fear. Never let them see your thoughts. Your face is your mask.*

"...of course, there's a chance that the wife *misplaced* it," Uuan was saying, tugging at the bottom of his long, wavy brown beard. Like many Brezhian men, he did not go grey in his advanced years, but his hair was a tad duller than a younger man's. Still, the deep-carved lines on his face gave no doubt to his age. Glannon figured the old man wouldn't last the winter if the crops didn't come in as they'd hoped, to say nothing for the cattle.

And here he was worrying about a cattle yoke.

"Uuan Loes," Glannon said, her voice strong and sure the way she had been taught. "I hear your petition, and I understand your plight. You accuse your neighbor Nerth Arvan of stealing your most prized cattle yoke, carved by your cousin Lou, and wish to seek the highest punishment—a new calf—in recompense for stealing."

"That's correct, Mormaer Bel," Uuan said, spinning his hat in his hands.

She considered the old man's options. The calf would be the easiest course of action. But Uuan had been here before, and she had read up on his previous grievances. He had a tendency for misplacing things, more so as he grew older, and a persecution complex. Outside the dark Cradle of Rule, where she performed the task of mormaer, it was sunny and bright. Autumn was in its last perfect glow, the light almost amber and the high grass of the fields beckoning her.

But, just as before her ascension to the position of mormaer, she had other, better, more important things to do. Was not her uncle ruler before her? And her mother before that? Nomina Bel was the greatest mormaer Bannercliffe had ever seen, and she had died in the Wothwood sacrificing herself to Noduuoret.

Glannon had earned her spot on the seat, and it was all she had ever wanted.

No one told her how boring it would be, though. How, in times of prosperity and wealth, the clan would resort to missing cattle yokes and accusations of impropriety and, worst of all, land disputes. Where gone were the days of rape and murder? Grand theft and assault? Raids to neighboring clans? Nomina Bel had taken the Coriou clan as her own during one brilliant night raid, and they still sung her song in the taverns.

But, like her mother, those days were gone. They went with Therian rule. No more raids, no more ships. No blood sport. All for a steady stream of grain and ale from the Continent and better trade. Neither came at regular intervals, and for the most part, Brezhians felt like third class citizens to the great Empire.

Glannon took a deep breath and said at last, not the words she wanted to say but those she knew she ought to say.

"Before I seek the maximum penalty for theft, Uuan Loes, I will send a small group of council members with you, three in total should do the job. They will question anyone in the area, including Nerth Arvan and his family, and also walk the premises on the slight chance that this yoke has been misplaced," she said.

Uuan was not pleased. The older ones rarely were. Per Sulcar said it was because so many of them knew her mother, had fought under her banner against the Coriou, and expected fire and brimstone and justice.

Glannon knew them by their scars. What the Coriou had wrought a generation ago was nothing short of butchery. Uuan was lucky to have both of his eyes and his hands, though it was rumored he walked with a wooden club for a foot.

"Very well, Mormaer Bel," Uuan said, and he turned to go after giving her a perfunctory greeting, fingers to his lips. "May the Goddess grant you health and long life."

Per Madoc breathed sharply at her side, and Glannon leaned over to hear his assessment of the situation. Unlike Per Sulcar, Per Madoc always had an opinion, and usually it was carved in stone before he opened his mouth. A fierce supporter of her mother's, and friend to her uncle, the blacksmith held the dual honor of being Glannon's right hand and her armorer. Not that she ever needed the latter.

"You could have just *given* him the calf," said Per Madoc. "Would it have killed you to relent?"

"Arvan is already a few steer short from the last time Uuan came petitioning, don't you recall?"

"I do," Per Madoc said, "of course I do. You are right in this matter, of course, as you are the goddess-blessed."

Per Madoc didn't really believe in the goddess, but he said the words anyway. Even if they were tinged with a bit of flat sarcasm. The seven pers were her closest advisors, but each held positions throughout Bannercliffe. Per Prigent was also the high priest, the emissary on Earth of the goddess Noduuoret, so it was rather required that he pay her living homage. It was she who had blessed Glannon's line, imbued them with strength of judgement and character, or so she had been taught. Noduuoret might have lived two thousand years ago, but her presence was still felt by many. Her burial ground, the Wothwood, stood an attestation to her power and might, the sacrifice she made for her people. Those who entered never returned. The fear of the goddess ran deep among her people, and she was revered greatly.

But not by all.

It was her mother, Nomina Bel, who had abolished the one faith—not because she did not believe herself, but because she found the thinking of

Bannercliffe to be surprisingly behind the times. Most of the other Brezhian clans had adopted the Therian pantheon to some degree or another, or at least folding Noduuoret in with them. She was very much like their mother goddess, Erisha, and so it made sense to assimilate rather than suffer the title of heretic. They were already considered barbarian as it was.

In Bannercliffe some refused the idea altogether, like Per Madoc. He believed that if gods and goddesses were so very different from culture to culture, then why believe in any at all? It was just proof of too much human meddling. Although many frowned at his approach, others still joined him. It was easy to tell who they were for they simply did not come to services or feasts. They did not preach against Noduuoret, for that would have been cause for distress, but they still grew in numbers.

And Per Madoc's nomination to the Circle of Pers had been no accident. Glannon knew well enough from the mistakes of her uncle that excluding the non-believers sowed anger among the ranks. There were few others as qualified as Per Madoc.

He was only ten years older than her but had a youthful quality about him, no doubt gained from hours at the forge. There was no other in Bannercliffe as doted upon by the young women, but as he approached his fortieth year, many were giving up on him. Either, they reasoned, he simply wasn't interested in a wife or, perhaps, he wasn't interested in women at all.

"Glannon?" he whispered.

He got away with calling her by her first name.

"I'm tired," Glannon said, squirming slightly as she noticed the next petitioner. "How many more do we have today?"

"Well, Uuan was your fifteenth petitioner. That leaves..." Per Madoc ran his fingers down the list, and Glannon could hear his skin scratch for a long while against the parchment. "Twenty-eight."

Bannercliffe was wreathed in darkness when Glannon finally left the Cradle of Rule. Her eyes burned with the strain of her duties, her head throbbed. Yet the rest of her body ached for running, for action. For fighting. Why had they spent all that time training her to fight, but never letting her? She had seven guards within a breath's distance every moment of her waking life.

She shuffled off after Yuri, the largest and most easily recognizable of her guard, and then heard Per Madoc behind her.

"Mormaer?" he called.

Glannon turned over her shoulder. For a reason she couldn't quite fathom, she flinched, as if expecting the per to strike her or stab her. The vision came in an uncomfortable flash.

"I'm sorry, did I frighten you?" asked Per Madoc.

"No," Glannon said, which was not true. "I thought I saw something in the bushes behind you. Probably just another owl. You know, Per Iarncar said that the foresters counted a record number of owl pellets on their last survey…"

Per Madoc was very handsome. He didn't let his beard get as long as most of the other men in Bannercliffe, mostly to prevent it from catching fire in the forge. Glannon was well past the age of marrying herself; she was not certain she was ready yet. Still, she couldn't help thinking about it when she looked at Per Madoc. During the day while she was working, she rarely had to look at him directly. But now he was standing just an arm's width from her, his height just a bit more than her own impressive stature.

Glannon, almost always steel-tongued, found herself babbling in front of Madoc more times than she'd admit.

"No one knows Bannercliffe better than you do," said Per Madoc with a grin. "But I did come to you with another matter. I was hoping you might visit me at the forge tomorrow, since there are no petitions."

"It's the goddess's day," Glannon said.

"Of course. And, although her worship has left my heart, I do still hold some of the same traditions. You need not come during the services, but after. I've a question. And a… proposition."

"You could have petitioned yourself," Glannon replied.

Per Madoc cleared his throat. "It is a matter that would require some discretion, and I am not yet prepared to speak of it to the village at large. Not until I've spoken to you, that is."

"I'll have to bring Yuri," she said. "And I'm not entirely sure I'll have the time. But I'll see what I can do."

Her heart skipped about in her chest as she walked away, and she thought she heard Yuri grunt in disapproval.

Late at night, while Glannon tried to sleep—something that often eluded her even after she was well within her cups—she would think about Braig Vann and what she had done to him when she was fourteen.

Fourteen.

She was older now, but every year marked felt a decade of weight on her shoulders. Not just from the guilt—though there was that, too—but from the responsibility of rule. Her decisions had cost men and women their lives, had taken children from their families, and resulted in more than a few lobbed fingers and, on one occasion, a hand.

The diadem was so heavy, but it was hers to bear.

Braig Vann was ill-suited for the job. Oh, they had loved him, doted after him, because he was so strong. How the villagers praised his muscles and his feats of strength. But Glannon was ever faster on her feet, more accurate with the bow and arrow, and, none would argue either, quicker with her wit. She was measured, even. She knew when to make the hard choices. Braig wanted to bed women and bleed men, much like his father.

Though she could never prove it, Glannon always suspected that Marchan Vann was behind her mother's death.

And there was the matter of the Feast of Nin, that night the year before Braig's father died. When he'd had been so drunk he'd tried to force his cock in her. Tore her dress, threw her up against the tree.

And the only way it didn't happen was more of that quick thinking on her part. She told him that the goddess would strike him down dead for sullying the day of her beloved's celebration, the Immortal Nin. And he had been afraid of that, at least. Not of what he would have done to her, or what it would have meant for them moving forward, but because he believed in some fanciful story. Or at least he did when he was raving drunk and drooling.

Before he let her go, he said, "Soon, when my father's done rotting from the inside out, I'll be mormaer. And you'll be my whore. Nothing you'll be able to do about that, Glannon Bel."

He'd never acknowledged it, not when they spent time together training again, or sitting across the banquet table. Braig seemed to have forgotten it, even when she offered hints to the events of the evening. He claimed he was too drunk to recall anything. But she could still feel his hand in her, under her dress, unbidden. She was a strong fighter, but in brawn no one in Bannercliffe had him beat. Many times she wished he'd be gored to death, imagined it in vivid detail.

No mormaer should be so faulted. No mormaer of such twisted character should be allowed to rule.

So when the day of the hunt came Glannon challenged Braig, she pressed him deeper into Briarwood. And she wished, prayed, more than anything, that a great boar would come to him.

And it did.

So, her prayer answered, Glannon Bel let Braig Vann die. The cut she had seen was beyond care, save for divine intervention. Leaving him had been the hardest moment of her life, but she survived.

Even if she had seen eyes behind him. A thousand ravens, beholding her from the darkening depths. Even if the dying boar itself was made of black wings and maggots. Even if the horror she felt said nothing but *wrong wrong wrong wrong.*

Because the Wothwood let her go, for reasons she had never quite figured out. She was not a pious woman; she did not hold Noduuoret close to her heart like her mother had.

So when she joined the hunting party, they had just felled another boar. The rest of the clan was so busy celebrating that it took a long time to realize Braig was even missing.

Still, they mourned Braig for a time, but with enough skirmishes and time, other young, able-bodied men died. Per Sklaer performed their last rites, burned their bodies, scattered their ashes in the fields so they would nourish the future harvests. The circle began anew.

Glannon became mormaer, and there was rejoicing because they had loved her mother and saw much of Nomina in her face and demeanor.

Except she missed her mother, every day. And cried at night because she was an orphan and had to carry the burden of the Bright Banner clan—the highest and most prosperous of all the clans—alone. And because when she had gazed into the depths of the Wothwood, her mother had not been there, waiting.

By the low-burning tallow candles, Glannon went over a handful of documents for the next day of petitioners. But her eyes swam before her, and she could hardly tell one story for another. Were Brezhians so stupid that they had to have someone else make decisions for them? What madness was this? A mormaer, in times of old, ran expeditions, commanded forces, inspired fear and awe. Now she was a nursemarm to two thousand with no end in sight.

Noduuoret, Per Prigent was always quick to remind her, brought peace to Brezhia when there was no hope left. When the beasts conspired with the spirits of the air and earth to break mankind. She gave up her sword, forged of the great star Berhed, and thrust it into the core of the world, silencing the dragons below and paying the blood price. Her great city was lost to her people, and she would never fight again, but in her peace there was judgement. The judgement passed down to every mormaer after, their duty.

But now, even some of the pers, like Per Madoc, didn't believe in Noduuoret. And if they didn't, why did she?

Glannon fell asleep under her thick furs, shaking off thoughts of murder and of godlessness, and wondering if they were connected.

She dreamed of black wings. Great beasts of many arms and faces, made of nothing but feathers, white and blue tipped and black. The feathers of the camulos owl, her family's sigil. It was a break from her usual nightmares, the ones about Braig Vann.

Per Madoc was right about one thing: Glannon knew Bannercliffe better than anyone. So when she made to meet him at the forge, she took a circuitous footpath between the bakery and the stables, under the guise of going to relieve herself—so as not to alert her guards—and found herself climbing in the back window to the forge, skinning her knees as she came down around the other side.

Just because she was mormaer didn't mean she had to follow the rules.

Truthfully, she didn't mind the sting. It reminded her of childhood. The wooden window jamb was rough, and it took off a good finger's width of skin across her knee and shin. But she didn't speak, didn't let a single sound come from her lips. In the next room, she could hear the forge bellows taking great, greedy gasps of air. It wasn't often that Per Madoc was smithing, due to the lack of resources. Most often he was glassworking.

She was in a bedroom. There was a narrow bed, cleanly kept; water jug for cleaning; a battered but clean chamber pot.

Glannon was about to inspect the desk when the large figure of Per Madoc appeared in the threshold. There was a subtle glow behind him from the forge, and he was out of his officiant's attire. It occurred to Glannon that she had never seen him in such a way before. His forearms were very strong, his simple shirt rolled up to the elbows. He wore the same leather kilt so common among her folk, and yet it seemed almost inappropriate on him, so used was she to seeing him wearing the long, brown robes of his station.

Any thoughts of baser matters, however, were quickly put to rest.

Per Madoc gave a sigh, as if Glannon's disheveled appearance and unusual entrance were mere bad behavior from a child.

"Glannon. I need to ask you a question," he said.

Glannon felt her insides go cold, like someone was rinsing her entrails. Like they did with the deer and elk they caught in Briarwood.

"Of course," she said.

Per Madoc took a step closer. Glannon had to resist the desire to shrink back. Usually, she was perfectly capable of going toe to toe. But something about Per Madoc eroded at her courage, and she felt very young, very small, and very out of her depth.

She noticed that the light from the forge made the small hairs on his neck alight, as if he were on fire as well. His eyes were dark, their surface shining ever so slightly, like wet mushrooms after the rain.

"Glannon Bel. Where is Braig Vann?"

Chapter Three
Deals

In Yereva, the tyckner population was common, but often overlooked. As the center of Therian life, the city was a natural melting pot, from the original inhabitants to the many conquered peoples of Luthland. Tyckners were important for their technological prowess. As a rule of law, the Elutil forbade the practice of metalwork to any of the Congregation. That included anyone born into the Mystery. Tyckners practiced a rather loose form of religion, if it could even be called that, that had no such restrictions. And since even the highest priests relied upon technology in some way—the grand clocks upon their bell towers, for instance—they had to make an uneasy alliance. More specifically, they worked as metal scavengers for the Elutil.

In Brezhia, it was a little different, though. Across the sea from Yereva, the wild and unruly territory of the Brezhians meant that the tyckners acted more as roaming mercenaries when needed, always ready to provide arms and sharpening should the needs arise. Various clans among the Brezhians had better alliances with the tyckners, or the Rovers as they were sometimes affectionately called.

Aoda had never seen their caravans up close before, though, as they were not allowed within the confines of Yereva. Tyckners could come through the gates with little wagons, their larger methods of transportation being banned, and they looked pretty much like the rest of the peddlers she was so used to seeing, save that they were a little more colorful, she supposed.

These caravans though, about three king's measures to the east, were not what she had expected. Aoda took note of their sturdy sides and structure; they looked more to her like log cabins, moving houses. Each was roughly of the same design: a long rectangle, kept together by a kind of wattle and daub between the hewn logs. They had cloth canopies on top of their slanted roofs of varying color, but mostly shades of purple, green, and gold.

The caravan was parked in a semi-circle, and the forges were out in force. Little children dressed in billowing tunics gamboled about playing some game with rocks and hoops, an old man in their midst. From what Aoda could tell, the goal of the game was to throw the hoop and then throw as many rocks into it as possible. There was a lot of shouting involved, and it was oddly punctuated with music. Someone was playing a lyre out of sight, madly and furiously, the notes coming faster than heartbeats. A woman sang lazily, missing half the cues, and laughing through most of the verses. It smelled of fried liver and offal, dank hay, and stale wine.

Tyckners were, on the whole, freckled and thin. Almost all sported tattoos of varying skill. They made their own clothes as a rule, and spared no expense. Their clothes reflected their worth in society, many with burnished buttons and bogglingly detailed embroidery. In fact, Aoda once recalled reading that the tyckners were known to bury their dead in favorite outfits, and that stealing a dead man's coat was a great offense—so great some had lost limbs or been put to death depending on the situation.

Either way, it was gaudy to Aoda's eyes, weak even as they were. The colors on their outfits clashed one against another, and it was hard to piece out where one's shirt began and hose ended. Skin, and the tattooed decoration upon it, was as on display as the cloaks and feathered hats and jingling belts.

The man who had been playing with the children—he was toothless with a long, pointed goatee—greeted Aoda and Shenbar as they approached. It was decided to send a smaller group out to see them, thereby giving Captain Moll a little time to calm himself down. It was no secret that he felt this assignment beneath him, and in moments of weakness, he made it apparent to everyone around him. Only Lieutenant Shenbar was able to keep him from brawling. And in some cases, that simply meant keeping him at a distance.

"We're here to see Sid Poole. Bozal the Bold said he might be here," said Lieutenant Shenbar, giving a somewhat awkward bow of acknowledgement. "Do you know if he's about?"

"I don't know what he's about, really," the old man said, smoothing out the front of his long buttoned coat. It was missing quite a few and was stained something fierce, but he carried it with a distinct sense of pride. "I don't suppose anyone but he does."

"He means we'd like to speak with him," Aoda added, bracing for the moment when the old man's eye met hers, narrowed, looked away in disgust.

But that didn't happen. The old man grinned at her. "Yeah. I imagine you do. Most people try, anyway. He's over there." One dirty thumb gestured toward the largest of the caravans.

"Thank you," Aoda said. "Sir?"

"Sir?" echoed the old man.

"The lady is inquiring after your name," Shenbar clarified.

Aoda felt her ears flush hot.

The old man took off his hat and brushed it below. "Beckham, as it were. Morse Beckham."

"Well, this here is Professor Aoda Kanna," said Shenbar.

"She can't introduce herself?" Beckham asked.

"Lieutenant Shenbar here is my superior," Aoda tried to explain, "so it's his duty to introduce me."

"But didn't you just introduce him, then?" Beckham asked, craning his tattooed neck back and forth. There were snakes drawn on both sides, striped and with long tongues reaching out toward his earlobes. The poor man was befuddled.

"It is a bit confusing, now that you mention it," Shenbar agreed, and then pressed on, Aoda at his heels.

Two guards greeted Aoda and Shenbar at the door to Poole's caravan, but they looked more perfunctory than truly dangerous. One was a big fellow with a surprisingly small head, his face newly bruised and a musk about him like a fermenting house. The other was tall and thin and carried a bow and arrow and knife, but looked more interested in what dirt had found its way under his nails than anything else.

Aoda knew better than to underestimate them, though. Lazy they might look, but the tyckners were known for prowess in battle.

"Evening," said the thinner one. He grinned showing a graveyard of yellowed teeth. "Here to see Poole, then?"

"We are," said Lieutenant Shenbar. "Sent here as an emissary from Captain Adamen Moll of the 31st Regiment of His Lord Re's Army in Brezhia."

"That's a mouthful," said the big one with the little head. "But we don't much like soldiers."

"This is a strictly peaceful assignment," Aoda insisted. "We are surveying the land for the establishment of a fort a little farther in the Wothwood."

It could have been her imagination, but Aoda couldn't help but notice Shenbar tensing a little at her words. As if there was something he didn't like about them. Or perhaps something he knew that could counter them. She'd have to remember that later.

The two guards looked to Shenbar for confirmation. "What the lady said," he said. "She's a better diplomat than I."

There was a moment's hesitation, but then without any further ado—and certainly far less pomp and circumstance than they'd ever been given—the rickety doors opened wide and they were given space to enter.

It was a difficult task finding the two men inside the caravan, for there was such an overwhelming amount of decoration within that Aoda could scarcely piece it together. The word garish fell flat. So did opulent, busy, discordant. Every surface was festooned with something, be it a button or a bit of crochet, a miniature painting, or a piece of taxidermy. There was quite a bit in the way of taxidermy, she noticed, much of which had been absorbed into the furniture. One chair had otter heads for arms and a bear head where one might rest their own. Table legs were haphazardly put together from animal legs to carved wooden stakes to, in one case, what looked to be some ancient Therian flail repurposed.

The walls were papered here and there, sometimes with sheaves of scrolls or books, other times with bits of embossed leather or, as in the case of a garish green portion behind what might have been a bookcase or curio shelf, a fresco, though stripped and stained beyond interpretation.

There were weapons, too, and books. Metal weapons, beyond valuable, but none remotely salvageable, so battered and full of holes were they.

Then there were beakers and flagons. Remnants of food. Wall-hangings, portraits askew here and there. Sculptures. Whirligigs. Half of a lute sticking out of the mouth of a boar head. And thousands of buttons. Buttons in jars, buttons in platters, in bowls, pinned to the walls.

Aoda had certainly not prepared herself for such a show of color and disarray, and it took her a moment to find her voice, let alone her feet.

Shenbar, standing stiff behind her, was unable to find words, either.

The skinny man sitting in front of them at the small table stood slowly, brushing the front of his ratty vest with his long-fingered hands. He was lean and freckled, his blue eyes buried a bit too deep in his sockets to be attractive. His nose had been broken a few times and took a steep twist to the right, and there was the remnant of a scar on his lips. He kept his long curls behind his head, down low in the old style, but carried himself well. As if he had no fear of these strangers.

And judging by the other man in the room, he didn't need to be afraid of them. The other fellow was positively massive. Not just in height but in physical power. Unlike the thin man, he didn't look like a tyckner, but rather a bit more like a shaved Brezhian in his features. He had a wide, handsome face, but one that had seen more than a few fights. The left side of his face showed a scar from temple to the side of his lip that could have meant a near fatality, a broken cheekbone, or worse. More scars reached up into his thick, auburn hair. His brows were dark as smudges of soot, but he wore no tattoos. Where the thin man wore typical tyckner clothing, this man had simpler garb. Leather, fit well to his body, made to protect him from attack should the need arise.

"Guests!" said the thin man. "Fancy guests. All the way from Yereva, I hear."

"Sid Poole, I presume?" asked Aoda. It was not the way she was supposed to address him, nor was it polite. But the tyckner didn't seem to care one bit.

"That's my name, or so's been since my mother squeezed me out of her fiddly bits," Poole said with a wide grin. "What might I call you?"

"This is Professor Aoda Kanna," said Shenbar, putting his fist on his chest in a common greeting. "I'm Lieutenant Ori Shenbar, and we're here to ask you some questions about Noduuoret's Grave."

Poole's thin eyebrows rose high. "As I said. Quite fancy. Hear that, Lon? They want to know about the very center of the Wothwood. Right in the middle. Noduuoret's Grave."

Lon said nothing in reply.

"We spoke to a man named Bozal," said Aoda. "He directed us to you."

"Of course he did," Poole said, hissing through his teeth. Not in a way of any genuine upset, but in a kind of amused disappointment. He was very showy, this Poole. Aoda had the strange sensation that, perhaps, she'd found her way into a play, and she was but a scene in the life of Sid Poole, an inconsequential set piece or bit player.

"If Bozal was mistaken, we can depart. We meant no offense, nor did we mean to waste your time," said Shenbar, playing the diplomat as he so often had before.

In other cities it worked.

"Waste my time?" asked Poole. "Lon, they think they're wasting my time! I hadn't thought about it that way, but now that you mention it, perhaps you can make it *worth* my time—my oh so very *precious* time—if you sweeten the deal. That's how all you Continentals deal with things, isn't it?"

Poole was of indeterminate age, but had a youthful way about him when he smiled. He spoke as if everyone was hanging on his every word. And at the moment, they were.

"You want money?" asked Shenbar, and Aoda could tell he was losing his resolve. This was down to the regular deeds. "I've got money."

Lon snorted.

"Money? We don't deal in money," said Poole. "We deal in *wealth*, which is quite another thing indeed. Look around you, Lieutenant. We hold the future of the world in our hands, our capable hands, because your ruling elite and their meddling Elutil believe technology, and every cog and wheel, to be but another step toward corruption. Do we look like a corrupt people to you?"

"No, you look like good, simple folk," said Shenbar, and Aoda winced internally.

"Simple," repeated Poole, shaking his head. "Always the mistake of your kind. You think that we are simple people since we don't mint coins and fashion ourselves kings and queens over land."

"Not all of us think so," Aoda said, her voice feeling so small even though it was coming from her throat. "Your work with metal—what little survives on the Continent—is the stuff of legend. And I see that you've got quite a store, here, too. You say you do not concern yourself with money, and yet the value I see here is as plain as day."

"My work requires that I have some metal to work with, and these are hard won," he said, gesturing to the swords on his wall. One, Aoda noticed, was down on the table, chunks of it removed as if it were Kargrian cheese. The tyckners were allowed to their metal work—all the gears and inner workings— but nothing larger than a button, so the Elutil had decreed—unless it was by their own sanction. It was rumored that they had a small village worth of tyckners locked up at the top of the Broken Tower in Yereva doing their bidding.

Poole looked at her with something like pity. As if he saw through one layer deeper than most folks managed. And it made her feel afraid. It made her feel exposed. She had begun to feel power in her ugliness, her wretchedness, because people ignored her. But not so with Poole.

"Then tell me, Professor," Poole said, leaning back and folding his arms as if he had hours to wait for the cattle to come in, "what do you see when you look upon the tyckners?"

She had been trying to find the sentiment herself. Unlike Shenbar, she did not mistake their wildness for chaos. There was a purpose in their order. Rules and socialization far beyond what she had learned or experienced in her life. University work was mostly rooted in mathematics and the teachings of the Old, but she had spent a little time in anthropology when the courses could suit her schedule. Tyckners were the only culture known in the Northern Half without a hierarchy or any kind—neither age nor wealth nor position could elevate another person over one another. So she had been taught.

Yet Poole was guarded and watched. He appeared to live in a caravan on his own, no wife or child or sign of family within the walls, in spite of the fact that the others looked fit to bursting. He was special.

There was a lot that she could say about Poole, Lon, and all the rest of them—even if she didn't believe Lon was a tyckner by birth.

"I see pride," said Aoda at last. "And knowledge."

Poole's eyebrows went up high, vanishing under his long hair a moment before returning again.

"Hear that, Lon?" Poole said, the sarcasm stripped from his voice. "That I did not expect."

"Will you help us, then?" asked Aoda. "It's a matter of great importance. Our survey will be the first of its kind."

Again, Shenbar looked a little uncomfortable at her mention of the survey.

"Yes, I think we can arrange something," Poole said, fingering his beard thoughtfully.

"You… have something in mind?" Shenbar asked.

The tyckner grinned, the smile spreading out and making dimples under his eyes. Then he stood, unfolding like a great grey crane, so that he showed his full height. Taller than Shenbar, far, far taller than Aoda.

He peered down at the lieutenant. "That's a very lovely coat you have, sir."

CHAPTER FOUR
HIRED MUSCLE

LON WAS A GOOD ENOUGH NAME. SHORT ON CHARACTER, EASY TO REMEMBER. That's what Poole said of it, anyway. It meant "boar" in old Brezhian. Sometimes, when Lon was sitting up late at night, polishing the tyckner spears that he carried as weapons, he thought about his old name, the name he'd used most of his life.

Braig Vann.

Glannon Bel and the boar had done away with that man, though. That *boy*, really. Seven years ago, Braig Vann was a big, self-centered lout who thought his future was as destined as the path of the stars across the firmament. Even if being mormaer wasn't his first choice of occupation, it was at least a decision made for him. He liked the idea that he didn't have to work like the other boys his age, didn't have to apprentice to be something useful. He was already imbued with the blessing of Noduuoret, and so he was destined.

Except, so was Glannon. Her mother had been mormaer before she met an untimely end, the role passing to her younger brother, Braig's father. And then, as the law went, to his firstborn son.

Braig Vann hadn't died at the edge of the Wothwood, which really was what he deserved. There wasn't much good about Braig Vann. And many times, Lon was glad to be done with him.

And now Braig Vann was just Lon. Lon the bodyguard. Protector of tyckners and their strange contraptions and stranger ways. Sid Poole had saved his life out there in the Wothwood, and he owed him a debt.

"Ten years or ten corpses," the tyckner had told him, his hand to the bleeding femoral artery. "Whichever comes first."

So far the count was seven years and just two corpses. The only good fighting to be found was on the Scabbard Coast, and that was a stop they only included in their journey every four years. Next year they were due again, and part of Lon liked the idea of killing some more of those pestilent pirates. He'd done away with two of them three years before, hungry for more blood—and the promise of freedom, whatever that would entail—but he knew the rules were a little more complicated. The corpses killed had to be a direct threat to Sid Poole. Killing at random to keep his tally high was both frowned upon and highly discouraged. Tyckners only used violence as a very last resort.

And Poole was often not at the caravan, leaving Lon behind and insisting that he could take care of himself.

"It's really an education for you," Poole always said. "Living like a tyckner changes you. And I knew you were ready for that the moment I laid eyes on you. No one ends up in the Wothwood, bleeding out next to a were-boar because of good choices. You're a symbol to me, a sign of hope for the future."

Now they were back on the eastern side of Brezhia, having had to circumvent the Wothwood. Not far from where he once lived and, according to most, died. And at the beck and call of bloody Therians, too. What a strange turn. Lon had dealings enough with them during his time with the tyckners, but sending this large a force to Brezhia for surveying seemed suspect to say the least. If he were still a Brezhian at heart, he'd have worried. But from what he'd heard, none of them wanted to help the Therians in the least, so it served them right.

Lon strode his circuit about the Therian camp for the sixth time that night, listening to the soldiers' chatter. There was little chance the Bright Banner clan would be out this far, and they generally did everything in their power to keep away from, as they called them, filthy roving tyckners. "Never trust a tyckner" and "crooked as a tyckner's soul" were phrases they frequently uttered in Bannercliffe, and most believed staying free of the nomads was the best course of action in life.

And Lon had felt the same way until Sid Poole saved his life.

Although he couldn't claim to have completely blended in with them, he had learned to live and think like a tyckner. It was all about movement, constant movement. Move with the seasons. Move with the tides. Move with the trends in trade, the rumors of war, the gem rushes, and the rise and fall of kingdoms great and small. They might have been called opportunist by some, but that was simply because others didn't understand. The tyckners needed no ancestral home because everything was theirs. They'd made their mark so far across the continent that even Therian language was steeped in tyckner speech.

"You know, they say the tyckners sprang forth from the great Field of Life, a corner forgotten but accidentally fertilized by the great bird god Mu-shen," said a voice, addressing him, presumably.

Lon turned around, surprised to have missed the previous part of the conversation.

It was the ugly woman, the professor, from the Therian envoy. Had she been reading his thoughts? Lon was no longer a religious person—the tyckners held no rules about their religion, which was said to have over two thousand gods, demigods, and demons with which to connect—but it still made the hair on the back of his neck stand up.

The woman, Professor Kanna he recalled, was sitting on a log, clasping a cup of something. It steamed subtly in the dark night air, enough light escaping from the distant campfire to bring the barest substance to it.

"You saying they're descended from shit?" Lon asked.

"I'm not saying it. I'd never say something like that," the professor replied, as if surprised he didn't know any better. "I am a scientist and a historian, and so I am bound by the laws of my discipline to seek out the truth with all the abilities given to me." She tapped the side of her head for emphasis.

He blinked at her. Something about the way she talked made him feel insecure. That forward falling talk, all the words spilling out in the right way, thoughts and ideas assembling too fast for him to interpret. Every response he attempted was clumsy in contrast.

He adjusted his spear. "Good on you then. Thanks for the education."

"But you're not offended because, as you just illustrated so clearly, you are not a tyckner," the professor said.

Lon couldn't say for sure, what with all that scar tissue about her face, but he at least felt her smirk implied. He'd walked right into that one, he did.

"You shouldn't care," Lon said, making his best effort to keep walking. But his ears were hot. His stomach felt as if he'd just got the bad end of the yoghurt batch.

"Oh, I don't. It's just that inconsistency intrigues me. It's where the stories are, where the truth lies."

"Ah, and what's the truth, then?" he asked, knowing she'd have the answer but unable to help himself. It had been a very long time since he'd spoken to anyone save Sid Poole.

"Everything that I've read indicates that it's quite rare for tyckners to take in people from other clans and cultures. Except when there is a blood debt. You look, more or less to me, like a Brezhian. Unlike the tyckners, I imagine you'd grow quite the beard." She paused, squinting and tilting her head. "And you speak Therian with just the slightest accent that gives away where you were born. It's a difficult turn of the tongue for anyone, but your fricatives are quite telling. The tyckners, in general, manage it quite well but struggle with the vowels more."

"You're a strange woman," said Lon. "And I've got a perimeter to check."

"It's the stubble that gave you away, really, or at least got me questioning," she continued, as if he hadn't said anything at all. "Put a beard on you and you'd be as Brezhian as they come. Bigger than average, but still."

"Please stop talking about my beard and my stature," Lon said. "It's inappropriate." He hated the pleading sound in his voice, but he didn't want this woman to keep talking. Especially down this line of logic. He felt like an ox on the auction block.

"I'm just doing my job. Observing," Aoda said. "But I'll let you do yours."

She leaned back on the log to get a better look at Lon as he passed, but he didn't think she could see him that well, even on a good day. He'd never seen such a poor excuse for a woman in all his life. Her face was a mess of bumps and spider web scars, her teeth misshapen, her eyes more of a suggestion than a reality. If she'd been born to the clans rather than in the great city of Yereva, she'd have been left to the wolves looking like that. He felt sorry for her.

"Look, I apologize," Lon said, not three paces past her. "People don't usually notice me so much."

"Ah, yes. Well, that's the opposite of my problem," she said. "People notice me far too much. I'd do anything for a plain face, really. Nothing remarkable at all. A blank slate upon which to write a future free of these scars." Aoda sighed, rubbing her hand down the side of her face. "But it is what I've got."

"Was it fire?" he ventured, squatting down across from her. "If you don't mind my asking." He fiddled with some bits of rock and twig strewn about the ground.

Aoda perked up, and she laughed brightly. "You know, no one ever asks me that. You're surprising, Lon-Who-Is-Not-A-Tyckner."

"I'm boring," he said.

"Doubtful. But, as I tell my students, all information comes with a price. Once you attain new knowledge, all shifts. Perspective tilts. And you are never the same."

"I can manage," said Lon. He liked her. In spite of her face, the way it moved so unsettlingly. There was a person behind that, a razor sharp wit, and a fearlessness he could admire.

"Mother is a prostitute," she said simply. "And, as such, carried a number of illnesses. One of them, the Walking Yellow Pox, did this to me." Aoda gestured to her whole face. "And if that wasn't bad enough, one of her upset clients threw acid on the side of my face when he found I was going to the Collegia. That took out most of the vision in this eye and attributes for the worst of the scars on the left side of my face. Seeing is difficult. And you've observed what it's done to me, otherwise. Many children born ill don't live very long, but Mother said I was always strong. And that's why she fought for me and put me through school."

Lon found, indeed, that the world shifted. He turned away from her slowly, no longer able to look her in the face. He was thinking of prostitutes and of Yereva, and the world he had only glimpsed from the back of a tyckner's caravan.

"And now you're here," he said, his voice low. "In the back woods of Brezhia, asking questions that make even the tyckners uneasy."

She shrugged. "It's my job. To take note, to ask questions, to…"

Aoda trailed off, and then stood suddenly. The other Therian he'd met in Poole's caravan was approaching, the lieutenant. Shenbar, if Lon recalled correctly. He wasn't bad as those folks went, he had to agree with Poole on that count at least, but he was hiding something. Shenbar's face was plain enough, but as the tyckners had taught him, Lon knew well enough that the lines of a man's body could give away more than their faces ever could. He was forever placing himself at angles to people, especially to Aoda. Especially when she went on about their peaceful mission.

Lon rather liked the idea of war. Looking at Shenbar, measuring him up, he suspected there would be a decent fight there. His face was good enough to look upon, but not without the signature of a man used to fights. That nose was broken at least twice, Lon figured, judging by the knob on the top. It sat between his thick-lashed eyes, cutting a just-so irregular line down his face.

"A lovely evening for a stroll," Shenbar said, stretching his back and smiling through his teeth. "Wouldn't you say, Professor Kanna?"

Aoda shrugged. "I was actually sitting," she clarified. "Lon here was just telling me about the wonder of the tyckner folk."

Lon had done no such thing, but he nodded because he sensed that's what Aoda wanted him to do. And for all his mental posturing, he knew on a base level that engaging in outright warfare with the Therians was unwise; they were vastly outnumbered. Though it would be good to smell blood on the earth again.

Shenbar's gaze shifted to Lon. "Has your master decided on a time table?" he asked. "I'm afraid we don't have much time…"

"He's not my master," Lon said, flatly. Now he was thinking of drawing Shenbar's blood again. Long and painful like. Maybe start by poking a few holes in his belly and see how he might squirm. Sometimes all you needed to undo a man was the fear of a knife in the belly. Then it was just a waiting game to see when they'd crack.

"Regardless," Shenbar said, clearing his throat. "I mean to speak with Poole as soon as he's charted our course."

"That's my job," said Aoda, more pointing out the detail for color rather than correcting Shenbar. "Once he's got his map drawn, I can superimpose it over ours and see how they work. Then we can go in."

"You… think that it's that easy, do you?" asked Lon.

"Is it not land?" asked Shenbar. "Is it not a forest? A thing nature made? The gods have given us ownership over all, and never yet have we encountered a land mass that would not bow to the army of Theria. We have ropes, we have artillery, we have manpower."

How much would they know? How much would he tell them? Growing up in Bannercliffe, he knew without a doubt that going into the Wothwood meant death. It was how Glannon's mother was killed. It was how he almost lost his life. The tyckners skirted it, flirted with the borders, and somehow they managed to stay relatively safe. But Lon couldn't help but imagine that the Therians were just walking straight to their deaths. The moment you crossed the Wo River, it was over. Whatever the goddess Noduuoret had done to save Brezhia, she had also doomed the Wothwood.

"You don't know the Wothwood like the locals do, Lieutenant. It's about more than manpower. If that's all it was, it would have been captured a long time ago," Lon said as evenly as he could muster.

"You don't say," Shenbar replied.

Aoda took up the strand of discussion, rescuing Lon from making a very angry fool of himself. "The Brezhians are a warlike, clan society," she said, straightening her spectacles. "They'd do anything for more land. Land is wealth and a sign of favor to their great governing goddess, Noduuoret. She was a famed warrior who gave up a storied career to settle as a kind of clan chieftain, a mormaer as they're called. And then she was purported to have gone into the area now known as the Wothwood to save her people and enter into a long time peace."

"Well, that certainly went over well," Shenbar said.

"The Brezhians were starving before that time, according to the records," said Aoda. "At very least they weren't, afterward. And her 'event' and the creation of her so-called grave times precisely with historical documentation regarding the Great Vanishment."

Lon felt sick. Hearing his entire culture described in such broad, academic strokes gave him the odd feeling of being a specimen for observation, stuck under a spyglass. Though Aoda certainly saw through him, he had some reservations as to whether or not Shenbar was that sharp. He seemed a man with his eyes intent on the horizon, uninterested in this last, remote bastion out on the outskirts of the Wothwood.

"But no one has even tried to get into the Wothwood?" asked Shenbar, sniffing the air, making an unpleasant face. "That's madness."

"Oh, people have tried," Aoda said. "There are nigh about twenty clans, and every few years or so, one of the mormaers has a dream, or is otherwise convinced, and goes out into the wood. But they never come back. It's said that they go to be measured by Noduuoret. If they are found lacking, they are not allowed to return. Or, alternatively, she is so enamored of them she keeps them as company. As such, everyone's forbidden to cross the river."

"But the tyckners," pressed Shenbar. "They've done it."

"To some extent," clarified Lon. "We know how to cruise the perimeter. There's rumors that some have made the journey and returned to tell the tale."

"And that's why we're here," Shenbar said, dismissing Lon with his hand as if he were as inconsequential as a fly upon the ass of a great horse. "There are inconsistencies I mean to suss out. I want answers, and maps, and results."

Sid Poole watched Lon with that measured, unknowable look of his. Even though Lon had given Poole an account of the conversation he'd had with

Shenbar and Professor Kanna, he'd conveniently left out the part where the professor had guessed his ethnicity.

"You're not going to try and stop them?" asked Lon when Poole said nothing more. "From going into the Wothwood, I mean."

"I have a theory," the tyckner said, holding up a long, knobbed finger. He had a vaguely sylvan look about him, as if his bones were made of wood. All his joints were thick and rounded, leaning toward bulbous the older he got. And that age was oddly indistinguishable. Early on, Lon had thought the man not much older than he was, but now he seemed a generation older. "I think it would be worth the trip for us."

"They just want to claim the land as their own," Lon said.

"Lon, your Brezhian is showing."

"They think the stories to be nothing but the myth of barbarians."

"And that offends you? I wasn't aware you were so pious."

"I'm *not*. They're just disrespectful."

"Of course they are. Theria was built on glass, and it can be sharp, but it is fragile. They do not want anyone to know this, and so they press on and on and on. Conquering and breaking the boundaries as they see fit, wanting to claim it all for themselves."

"They're godshitting monsters," Lon said.

"Yes, but this, Lon, is why the life of a tyckner is so freeing. We own nothing. We make no attempt to own or control. We move with the wind, and we form what we find into magnificent pieces of technology. We change the world, and our lives, not by staking claims and waging wars, but by simply creating. We have no allegiance but to learning, to craft. I had hoped that you'd come around to seeing that, but I have my doubts."

"We were talking about going into the Wothwood," Lon reminded Poole. "Not about tyckner philosophy."

Poole had a habit of allowing his thoughts and speech to eddy about during the course of conversation. It took Lon years to realize when to reel it in and when to let it go. Tonight he knew he had to keep Poole focused.

"Yes, I suppose you're right," Poole consented. "But my aims and theirs might have some surprising connections. You know we take a great interest in the Wothwood, we tyckners."

"You take interest in owl turds, too," Lon pointed out. "You're interested in anything that comes along your way. That's just how you do things."

Poole frowned. "Wothwood is important to me, Lon."

"They already think you're inconstant and unreliable; it wouldn't be smart to prove them right."

"And why not? I am both of those things," Poole pointed out. "And I want to keep them believing in my shortcomings because it will serve me well in the end. The truth, Lon, is that we've considered going deeper into the Wothwood for a very long time, but we have been reluctant to do so due to the rather challenging political climate. There are resources, mineral ores, useful inroads that our people could use to a significant advantage. I have pieced together more than I will unveil to the Therians."

"I don't follow."

Poole leaned back, steepling his fingers. "Oh, Lon. It's called an ulterior motive. And I'm trusting you to trust me in this matter. I have little hope that our Therian friends will make it out of the Wothwood alive, but that's because they are there for the wrong reasons. To rape it. To destroy it. We, on the other hand… have other business."

"I assume it's classified."

For a moment, Poole almost looked sad. Then he brightened, winking. "When the time is right, I will bring you into the mystery, Lon, usher you through the gate of my thoughts. For now, make sure no one tries to kill me. The last thing I need right now is a spear in the chest."

CHAPTER FIVE
FORGED

"I don't care where Braig Vann is," said Glannon, staring down Per Madoc. If he meant to scare her, she wasn't having it. "He's dead, either attending to the Night Bear or at the right hand of Noduuoret. Or, more probably feeding the worms."

Per Madoc kept her gaze for a moment, then nodded.

Every day since she'd left him to die, Glannon had thought about Braig Vann. His name sometimes sounded in her head like a bell, over and over again. At first, it came with a deep guilt. And though it hadn't gone away entirely, it was so familiar and private that to hear his name come forth from Per Madoc's lips made her feel ill.

She had believed, had accepted as fact, that he was dead and that not a single person in the entire clan suspected her of such ill deeds. They had only mourned Braig for a short time. His mother had died years before when the pox came through, killing lots of folks. Even Glannon's little, unnamed baby sister. When Braig died, there was no one to wail for him. As the custom was, one year and a day from his disappearance, he was considered dead to the clan. They lit a pyre for him and commissioned him to Noduuoret.

But Glannon was no fragile woman; she was tempered in the fires of Noduuoret. She was made brilliant and beautiful and clever, born into this position, the same as Braig. He'd had the brawn, but she's always had the speed of body and wit. Her mother had known, before she'd gone into the Wothwood, that Glannon would be mormaer someday. And it had come to be.

"He was a big lad," Per Madoc said. "About your age, a few years older, wasn't he?"

"I suppose so," she replied.

It was truth. She kept her face still, she relaxed her shoulders, she stilled her breath. The truth flowed through her. It would save her.

Per Madoc took a step sideways, then gestured her into the warm room beyond, the forge already at capacity. It smelled of smoke, flux, and the morning light cascaded in, flecked with dust and particulate, shimmering.

"We Brezhians don't like to speak of the dead, it's true," Per Madoc said as Glannon passed by him. "But I'm not your usual Brezhian. Braig would have been a warrior of the likes we'd never known in Bannercliffe. Perhaps not the brightest, but remarkably strong and cunning in the ways of war. Such a waste of life, in the end. I imagine he got lost in the Wothwood and then ate a poisoned fruit. Such is the way of that place, so I hear. Full of poison."

She half expected an ambush in the room beyond. But there was no such thing. Simply a neat, well-appointed space, dirt floor smooth and clean, the trappings of the trade—weapons and pieces of weapons—piled about the room in various states of completion. There were few better glass-smiths in all of Brezhia, and Glannon wondered if that was even a modest sentiment.

Something caught her eye, and she saw Yuri in the window pane, his ugly face distorted more than usual by the wavering glass.

She was relieved that he'd found her, even when he shook a finger at her. She had to make his job more of a challenge. Usually she was in a more playful mood. Today, she was not.

"Or the Wothwood chose him and the curse enacted its revenge," she said.

Per Madoc grinned, his eyes crinkling at the edges. "Yes, of course. Though you understand, as a man of reason, I must look for explanations outside the realm of the supernatural. Anything can be a weapon. Anyone, really."

Glannon swallowed as Per Madoc crossed the room and took out a long, simple box, the sort that she had seen sword merchants carry around.

He smoothed the top of the box and said, "When Braig met his fate, oh, nigh on seven years ago now, if you'll recall, I was no per, but a simple smith's apprentice. We'd been commissioned to make that great big man a great big sword, in celebration for his ascendance to the Chair of Rule. We didn't have much in the way of metal, but we used what we could."

Glannon watched, focusing more on her breath and keeping still her mind than truly taking in Per Madoc's words.

With soot-stained fingers, Per Madoc unlatched box and opened it. Whatever was inside—presumably a weapon of some important make—was covered by a long, white fur stole.

He continued. "After Braig died, and my master soon after, I was supposed to destroy the work. It is considered unlucky to give away a weapon to another, but I could not bring myself to do so. I had taken a long time, and your family—for you both come from Old Ruse—had invested a great deal in the forging of this enormous sword. It would have been magnificent. Besides, I don't believe in curses."

Glannon licked her lips, took a step closer.

Per Madoc pulled back the white fur to display two narrow, perilously sharp swords. They were similar to the long glass-bladed daggers she'd used day in and day out during her training, but they shone like starlight. Even without touching them, she could feel how cold they were, could see the fine etching upon the blades. Feathers. A burst of them up and down, as if they had been taken by the wind. They were the same kind of blades her mother had, the same she'd carried into the Wothwood.

The same feathers in her dreams.

She felt the hair stand on the back of her neck seeing them.

"Your mother had a set, much like these, of course, but they were lost with her," said Per Madoc. "I had thought the schematics lost, but a few months ago while I was cleaning out the last of Cormac's effects, I found the original schema for the kando blades, his own design of course. And I had not destroyed the massive blade I was working on for Braig Vann, so I decided—since you are the true mormaer—it was yours by right."

The *true* mormaer. The way he said it...

"You're not saying anything," Per Madoc said, a note of hurt in his voice.

Glannon found her mouth had gone dry. She was pulled toward the kando blades, wanting to touch them more than she had wanted to touch anything. Knowing that the grips would feel perfect in her hands, knowing that she would never want to let them go.

"But I am a mormaer of peace," said Glannon, clasping her hands behind her back to prevent herself from snatching them up. "It's been said, time and again by the council that there is no need of me to wield weapons of war. We are not at war. Marchan Vann issued the treaty with Theria and now..."

Per Madoc turned away from her and picked up one of the kando blades, slid his finger down the shaft. He did not look jealous of the weapons, but Glannon thought he looked a little sad.

"The time of peace is over, Glannon Bel, and there are strangers going into the Wothwood. Others who would take the place from us," Per Madoc said, not looking at her. Still staring at the knives, still running his fingers along the blades, impervious to their biting metal.

"Others?" Glannon asked, the idea both thrilling and terrifying at the same time.

"You know from our missives that three small battalions of Therians landed two weeks ago. One of them has been behaving unusually. They are going from town to town as they have done in seasons past since the Peace, but now they are asking questions about the Wothwood. Asking for Brezhian guides to take them through, and offering a pretty sum. More than a pretty sum. Three days past they sent word that they wanted to speak to you directly."

Glannon's temper flared and she scowled at Per Madoc. "And you didn't bother to tell me this?"

"You had pressing matters. I took the issue to the pers, and they agreed—unanimously—that we ought to decline their invitation. I took it a matter further and sent a few men out to the next village seat to see what would happen. And lo, good old Bozal Osca of the Seven Leaves clan came to me late yesterday confessing a great error on his part," Per Madoc continued, now holding out the kando blades to Glannon.

It was as if they were performing two parts of a dance, one in which they were talking politics, and another in which he was giving her a great gift. There were other words implied than those that she spoke, a countermelody to the discussion at hand.

"Bozal didn't agree to take them, did he?" said Glannon, remembering his penchant for fiddling his fingers through his long beard in the most grotesque way.

"No, but he's done something worse. He claims he didn't think that old Poole would ever be up to it, but it seems something the battalion is up to piqued his interest enough."

"You mean Sid Poole? The tyckner?" She knew him by reputation, everyone did, though she'd never had the occasion to meet him.

Now she wondered if she had made the right call with her lax approach to the tyckners. She pitied them and felt guilty for the way her people had treated them in the past, often using them as target practice or setting their caravans on fire. If they were helping the Therians while her own people were not...

"One and the same," said Per Madoc. "And by rights, as the mormaer of the Bright Banner clan, you alone are given this task above all others. *Should others enter unto the holy ground of the Wothwood, Noduuoret's great bower, woe to them, for the mormaer of Bright Banner shall bring wrath to their ranks.*"

"I didn't think you believed in the Song of Noduuoret. Or Noduuoret at all," Glannon said.

Her hands were before her again, hovering over the hilt.

"I don't need to. Your people do. And were you to shirk this task, there would indeed be questions asked," Per Madoc said. "Should this be your fate, then you need not hesitate. I may not believe in the goddess the way that most of the people here do, but I do believe in duty. And honor. And fighting for that honor when pressed."

His keen eyes leveled at her. He didn't need to say it, and Glannon didn't need to acknowledge it. But they both knew. There was a name that stood between them, and an accusation. But the keen blades before her would sort that out soon enough. She would prove to Per Madoc that she was destined for this.

Trial by combat. It was what Glannon had prayed for, begged for, since the moment she was old enough to fight on her own. Since she'd humiliated Braig Vann and her other cousins and peers in the training ring. Before she'd been made mormaer, tamed, and put aside. It was why she had never stopped in her morning drills. Why every morning she bore pain in her side and in her legs and pushed on, and pushed everything else away. And focused…

Because she knew. On some level, she understood that someone would challenge her. Someday. And she had to be ready. She had the name and she had the talent, but she had walked into her rule under curious circumstances. And though no one had wanted to press her then, times were changing. The Wothwood was her demesne. And she would have to prove her mettle, once and for all.

She reached out and wrapped her hands around the leather hilt of the kando blades. First one, then the next. It was warm already, perhaps by virtue of having sat near the forge for so long. But the transition was like touching the skin of another human being, supple and yielding and perfect.

"Then we ride," she said. "We ride to prevent these strangers from entering the Wothwood, and we take with us our best, we bring together the Kestenn— Togo and Caxigo, at the lead. Yuri, of course. And Per Carro, to help us develop the strategy. We'll have to tread carefully as not to raise suspicion, of course, but that will be well worth the risk…"

Per Madoc smiled at her as she began moving around the room, testing her blades, swinging large arcs, and never stopping in the conversation at hand. She had become one, whole. A woman, a purpose, and her blades. Now, she just had to figure out how a troop of two dozen Brezhians would manage to stop an army of two hundred from marching to their certain deaths.

If that was even what she wanted to do. She hadn't yet decided.

There had not been a muster of this size in over twenty years. It was the second year of her mother's reign when the Kestenn were assembled last, but Glannon barely remembered it. She recalled the height of the spears towering over her head like great oak branches, or the pikes of a fort, their tips glittering with sharpened points. She remembered the faces she knew—the farmers and craftsman—turned harder, brighter somehow, with these new vestments.

The Kestenn didn't bother with the kinds of armor favored by the Therians. It was an old adage around Luthland, but it was true: the forest was all the armor a Brezhian needed. It was said that the Freewood, the Briarwood, and the Wothwood were the final resting place of three dragons, and their scales nourished the trees, their blood fertilized the landscape, and Noduuoret herself blessed the connection between the trees and her people.

So it was that the Kestenn fashioned their shields to look like the bark of trees: roughhewn at a distance but carved and formed by masterwork craftsmen, aging the wood for centuries in caves to get a near impenetrable surface. The same method was used on their coats of mail and to bolster their leather armor.

Now, as she rode at their front, accoutered in the mail of Noduuoret—a white wolf pelt over her helm and a glittering belt made of burnished tortoiseshell—Glannon felt her heart beating more wildly than it had ever done before.

These were her men and women. Her warriors. The Kestenn were, much like the pers, village members. They were bakers and mothers, husbands and farmers, across all sections of Brezhian society. The only difference was that they were required an hour of practice every day to hone their skills and had done so since the age of twelve. It was at that age, her people believed, that the soul was truly formed. Some of the Kestenn were born fighters; others became fighters. But they were all deadly. It had been rumored that if the Brezhian clans had united their Kestenns together, Theria would never have been a threat at all.

The Kestenn of the Bright Banner clan, though, they were the most storied of all. True, all mormaers were considered equal, but that was merely in the eyes of the law. In the eyes of people, which is something else entirely, the strength of the clan name went far and wide. Perhaps only White Scale clan could pose a challenge to the Bright Banner, and only because their line of mormaers had gone on interrupted for three hundred years at last count, from parent to child, one line unbroken.

Yuri was not a Kestenn himself, but he had trained many a day with them. As part of the mormaer's bodyguard, it was his duty to work with them on drills, in the case of a raid—which had not happened since Old Ruse's day, but was done for the sake of tradition—or some other unpleasantness. He nodded his oval, neckless head in their direction as they passed Glannon.

Per Madoc, Per Carro, and Per Sulcar would accompany them from the Circle of Pers. Per Madoc was a natural choice, picked more for his skill as a smith and less for his involvement with the mormaer's affairs. Per Iarncar oversaw the foresters, and as such was a skilled tracker and student of herb lore. Although they did not plan to enter the Wothwood directly, there would likely be need of someone who knew the land to such a precise degree. Last came Per Carro, balanced on a skittish mare. Per Carro was a master tactician and a seasoned warrior with a penchant for understanding how to break down an opponent in body and soul.

"It's a good group," Yuri said, checking his immense steed at her side, the long dyed fur swishing back and forth in rhythm.

Glannon tried to keep her face placid, but she broke and had to hide her face behind her hand. "It should do the trick," she said. "But I suspect your presence will bring us half the way there. You look terrifying in your full garb."

The bodyguard grinned, showing his missing teeth. "Aye, and I get uglier every day, so says my sister Uula."

"Fear is half the battle, so my mother used to say," said Glannon, remembering her mother's face, vague as it grew every passing year since her death. She would have given anything for a sibling that bore her resemblance, or otherwise more features that reminded her of her mother's face.

In a moment like this, prepared to speak before the muster of Kestenn, she wanted to see her mother's eyes, to mark the lines and the crinkles on her cheeks. But the Wothwood had taken that from her, just as it might take her own face, her own life. That was the fear, was it not? That if they could not convince the tyckners and the damned Therians to stay out of the Wothwood, they'd have to go in after then. And then…

"Well, I've got that in spades. But I'd warrant that most of the Kestenn could give me a run for my life. Take Caxigo. That woman's no one to fuck with, not even a little. I've seen her footwork, and her mastery of the old style. You've got no deadlier one among your ranks," Yuri observed, pointing over at Caxigo.

The woman was standing at the end of the line of muster, her flaxen hair braided and tucked up inside her helmet. There were so many freckles upon her cheeks that she almost appeared a shade darker than the rest of the muster, most of that garnered from years working the farm in the sun. But she stood as tall as most of the men, and broad besides. She'd born four sons, all of whom were no older than seven summers, but her husband Mogan did most of the child rearing, as was often the custom with women in the Kestenn. Mogan was a large man, almost as big as Yuri, but he had not been born with a fighter's heart. When the call came, he was unmoved by the goddess. Instead came Caxigo.

Glannon imagined that Caxigo wasn't that much younger than her own mother, knowing they spent summers together in training. Her own mother had been married very young, and she was born soon. Caxigo had taken her time to find the right match, and Mogan was from the Seven Streams, an allied clan. He would do right by her, as far as Glannon knew. There had never been an argument raised against him, never a complaint.

"I'll keep her close," Glannon said.

"Mormaer!" came a voice from behind her. Per Madoc.

"Yes, Per Madoc," she replied, evenly as she could manage.

"It is time for your speech," he reminded her.

Yes, she'd worked that bit out. For all her fighting prowess and her sharp mind, it was her tongue that Glannon Bel valued most. It was what swayed men, what stayed weapons, and stilled hearts where cold steel could not. It was, they told her time and again, like the very voice of Noduuoret, echoing again through the ages.

Her steed picked up pace, and she calmed the stout animal, smoothing her hand down its curly mane. It had been a long time since Grig had seen this many other horses, and the beast was growing a bit anxious.

Still, with a little guiding, Glannon had Grig moving along at a good canter. She raised her blade high and let out a sharp cry. All those who, until that moment, had been lost in their own thought and the general din of the muster, came to as they watched their mormaer take to the front, dazzled.

This was her finest moment. The moment she had been born for, the realization of her mother's dearest dreams. The waking of the goddess within her.

Chapter Six
Briarwood

In her twenty some-odd years, Aoda Kanna had experienced plenty of fear and uncertainty. Growing up, as she did, as a brothel rat, it was not uncommon to be beaten or chased for reasons she never quite understood, other than being at the wrong place at the wrong time. The world was full of men and women bigger and stronger than she, with smoother faces and more influence. Their hands and tempers strayed in ways she would never be allowed.

But in that time, she also learned she had advantages. She was smarter than almost everyone she knew. She had an aptitude for details, for remarking on things about people that they may not even notice.

Once, Aoda got her mother out of significant trouble by remembering that she'd smelled a smear of fig paste on the shirt of one of the brothel owners. She'd procured a jar of the precious stuff—nearly emptying out all her meagre savings at the time—and gave it to him as an apology from her mother. Her mother certainly never would have done such a thing, prideful as she was, but Aoda was concerned about her life. The man gave up his threats after that, not due to the bribe, necessarily, but likely because the fig paste itself had been seeded with nettle, and he'd developed a rash both around his mouth and down his throat which, to most, looked like he'd gotten pig rot, that disease well-known to those keeping intimate company with pigs.

He left the brothel soon after and did not call upon the women there.

Details. Yes. Aoda had always feasted on details. They were the bits and pieces of existence that too many people forgot. Individually, they didn't matter much at all. But put together, they were powerful. The sum of the way a person saw a world could be seen in their details.

Captain Moll's details said he wanted to be done with this forsaken trip, done with everyone in the camp, and done with work. He was restless. He asked the same questions over and over again. And even when they'd made great progress through Briarwood, going faster and farther than they had planned, he was impatient and curt with everyone, even Lieutenant Shenbar. Just an hour before, he had shouted at the man when his horse had loosed a shoe. In this cold, strange environment, it was no surprise and no infrequent occurrence.

Aoda didn't want to love Captain Moll. She knew she was attracted to him for every wrong reason, and she could never let herself fully detest him. Just when she thought she was able to wash her mind of the more sordid thoughts of him and start anew, she would be reminded of why she couldn't by the way he smiled or laughed. It wasn't fair of her to feel that way, especially when he bullied Shenbar, who was always the first to recognize her talent and defend her.

Still, she found herself pining from behind, riding beside Shenbar as they made ready for camp.

"It's hard to get used to, isn't it?" Aoda asked him when the company halted at dark.

They had spent about two hours waiting for the tyckners to return, a few of them having gone out in front to do some scouting. The Wothwood was not far, but they wanted to be sure nothing was out of the ordinary. Shenbar had allowed for this as a measure of trust, but certainly disagreed with it on matter of principle. If they were ahead of schedule, they should keep it that way.

Shenbar looked behind him and then down, spotting the professor and nodding in acknowledgement. "Which part? The air that is somehow cold and yet thick? The trees that smell of rot and disease? The forever hungry bugs?" To punctuate his irritation, he slapped at something on his neck.

"They're called cheer flies," Aoda said.

"What an ironic name."

"They thrive in the cold weather, one of the only sort that manages such a feat out here. We've been slowly gaining altitude, the Wothwood itself is on a kind of plateau, and once we're up a little higher, the bugs will be gone. But horse is their favorite dish, whenever they can get it. It's why the Brezhians breed such wooly ones."

Shenbar sighed, checking his tack one last time before turning to face Aoda a bit more squarely. "Your ability to remember every detail of this place never ceases to amaze me, Professor," he said.

"I've been collecting my observations for the trail guide," she said. "To make sure the next company through is better prepared than we are. We wouldn't want them making the same mistakes. And while we've not been able to speak to the Brezhians as much as I'd like, considering they're the ones who've lived here for ages, I have gleaned quite a sum of knowledge from the tyckners on local herbs and lore."

There was that pause again. Shenbar might have thought he was being clever about the whole business, but he was underestimating Aoda considerably. There were only so many pauses one made in responding to a subject before it became suspect. And the pauses got longer the deeper they got into the Wothwood and the more private conversations he had with Captain Moll.

Then Shenbar said, "The next company?"

"The one the Lord Re is sending," Aoda continued, recalling her conversations with Captain Moll back in Yerevan. They were to clear the way, that was always the plan. "Once we've done the survey, they'll arrive. The one with more scientists and engineers."

He was going to say something more, to clarify just what it was that she hadn't told him since they left. She knew it. She could see him preparing to deliver the truth. She'd already begun to feel relief that the lie between them was going to dissipate. Aoda hated when she knew she was being misled. It was like having a persistent boil on your foot and being forced to walk a mile. Yet it was not enough to guess at it: she wanted to hear it from Shenbar, she wanted to know he trusted her.

But just then, the camp came alive.

Strange how Aoda had just been thinking about Brezhian steeds, for that was what began to pour in from all sides, expertly commanded by a most impressive Kestenn, banners flying and voices rising high. Seventy, maybe more. They came in every color and looked almost like enormous sheep, their long floppy coats shaking long after they came to a halt.

Then came the hounds. Half as tall as the horses, standing still as statues as they came to a halt with a high-pitched whistling commands. Coarse-haired, long-nosed, bred for the purpose of bringing down boar and elk and the stray shaggy bison on the island. Their black eyes twinkled in the firelight, ready for action at the slightest command. Each member of the Kestenn had two hounds to their name, their leads as they were called, selected from their personal pack to attend to the muster when called.

There were spears, too, glass glinting deadly. The warriors looked like the two soldier castes she recalled, the Kestenn and the foot soldiers. They were tall and proud, far better rested than her own Therian troops. She vaguely recalled the face of the of the pers that she noticed and tried to recall the page in her notes. Per Madoc, she remembered, seeing his name as she'd written it down, recalling that theirs was a clan run by a relatively young woman named Mormaer Bel. Aoda had not had the chance to speak to her, since Per Madoc had insisted they be on their way and would not offer any help to them, as he should have as a Therian citizen.

But the look on Captain Moll's face, now. That was something else. He was focused on the woman riding on the whitest of all the Brezhian steeds, her long dark hair braided down over her shoulder and a winged helm on her head. He seemed surprised at her beauty, for it was apparent indeed. Yet it was not the kind of beauty one would expect in Yereva. Her nose was too large, her chin a bit too weak. But her eyes burned with something akin to starlight as she looked down upon the small battalion. Aoda had never beheld such an imposing woman.

"I am Mormaer Glannon Bel, called by Noduuoret as protector and judge to the Bright Banner clan!" she cried, holding aloft one of her swords. Kando blades, forged of true steel. "I come to you, just a half a day's ride from the border of the Wothwood and the crossing of the Wo River, to do my duty and prevent you from entering this heinous place. Who is the leader among you?"

Captain Moll held out his hand, staying the swords of the few tired and surprised soldiers nearby. Without the tyckner presence, their company was even less impressive than it would have been, given the situation. They may have been a more modern unit, but after the series of wars of the last century, not a single one of them would underestimate the power of a Brezhian Kestenn.

There was fire in his eyes, too. Aoda had mistaken his gaze for lust—it was something else, now. He was ready. He wanted this fight.

"I am Captain Adamen Moll," he said, "second son of Lord Gor Namzu Moll of the Seventh Province. I command this battalion by order of the Lord Re, Most Mighty Sovereign of Yereva, Shesh-kalla. We are here under his orders."

It was the first time, Aoda observed, that Captain Moll didn't add any falsities to their purpose. No mention of a survey. No discussion of a peaceful mission. And while she had been expecting this to come to the surface soon, Aoda still felt a chill run through her. She had traveled so far with Shenbar and Captain Moll, become so accustomed to their routine and their scripts, that to hear him deviate made her shiver.

Aoda didn't like being suspicious. Especially of people she found herself so drawn to, like Captain Moll. But a quick glance at Lieutenant Shenbar and she knew he was out of his depth, too.

Had they been waiting for this all along?

"I hesitate to shed blood in this place," Mormaer Bel said, and some of her Kestenn grunted behind her as if they did not agree with this sentiment. "But I see you fingering your blades and contemplating how best to break our ranks. I'll tell you that blood on the ground will only call the creatures of the Wothwood to you, drawn by the smell and the promise of fresh meat. Our people have lived here time out of mind, protecting this border, respecting the lines drawn by nature, preventing the Wothwood from growing and taking over the mainland."

Aoda felt her hair rise on the back of her neck in spite of the fact she knew this discussion to be utter nonsense. The Brezhian clans were staunch fighters, true. But they didn't have much to offer to the rest of the Therian Empire other than the woodlands—many of which were being depleted at an alarming rate. As a culture, they were perilously tribal, notoriously insular, and generally speaking, barely better than savages. They built no great cities, they made no remarkable crafts, they told stories akin to those known the continent over. That they guarded the Wothwood, both rich in timber and, if her research proved right, much more besides.

She knew that the sources pointed not just to wealth, but the possibility of a city, an old remnant of the ancient Brezhians. She mentioned as much to Shenbar a few times, but he did not seem convinced. Almost no one believed the stories anymore. Oh, there were plenty of hints in Brezhian lore, but many scholars claimed to believe the concept of their ancient city to be merely a metaphor for their dwindling hold on the region. Either they were keeping its location to themselves, or they had other reasons to be so protective of the place, even if they did not venture in.

The power of a story can be remarkably strong on the minds of the weak, her mother used to say. It was how her mother would woo men to her bed. They believed her words, her story, even if it wasn't true, and they bought into that dream dearly.

"All very impressive," said Captain Moll, sweeping his eyes across the gathered muster once again, sizing them up, but in his casual, almost friendly manner. He was outmanned twice over, and at a significant tactical disadvantage. "But I am afraid that I have the seal of the Lord Re himself, here, and you will be hereby named traitor should you prevent us from doing our duty. It was divine inspiration that turned the Lord Re's eye upon the Wothwood, and we must do his bidding."

To her credit, Mormaer Bel did not look as if she was in the least swayed by this talk. She pressed her lips together as the man to her side, Per Madoc, leaned over and said something. She nodded almost imperceptibly.

"I am told you have sought the help of tyckners," she said. "But I do not see them here."

"They are scouting ahead, and you are changing the subject," Captain Moll replied, grinning.

"We have an ancient alliance with the rovers," she said, "and were they to aid you in this, we could no longer offer them our protection. Our ties go back further than those to Theria."

"I hear your 'ancient alliance' has included practicing raids on moving caravans and setting them afire," the captain said. "That hardly seems like a worthy alliance."

Glannon Bel frowned. "I do not excuse the acts of some of my lesser brothers and sisters, but I promise no harm will come to them under my watch."

"No doubt, great lady," said Lieutenant Shenbar, coming forward and pressing a hand to his chest, the sign for peace. Aoda felt relieved the moment he spoke. Captain Moll wanted blood, and the only way to convince him otherwise was to provide a better alternative. "But you must understand their position, as well. We have given them the opportunity to make history. To be part of the first survey team into the Wothwood in over three hundred years."

"Who are you?" asked Mormaer Bel, narrowing her eyes.

"Lieutenant Ori Shenbar," he replied. "Son of Belanum."

"Tell me, Lieutenant Ori Shenbar, Son of Belanum," said Mormaer Bel. "Our names sound like kin, though I know we are not. So speak wisely to me, openly. When you look upon my Kestenn, what do you see?"

"Proud, fierce warriors, ready to defend their land," said Shenbar, his voice as still and strong as ever.

"Do you not doubt that we understand that signs and portends from your Lord Re are simply the packaging on your true purpose, the same purpose of all those who have tried to take Brezhia and failed? We know well that there are purported riches, and a great city besides. But those who go in never return," Mormaer Bel said.

"Strange you mention that because, although all your fellow Brezhian brothers and sisters spoke to the same concerns, I was not able to get a single tale from them—nothing more than unsubstantiated myth, of course, and anecdotal evidence," Captain Moll said, the edge of his lips lifting in a grin. He had been thorough, Aoda had to at least give him that credit. He was not boasting. The Brezhians were all afraid of the Wothwood, but they never gave any indication that they had experienced its peril. "Oh, Bozal so-and-so knew someone's whore who thought their uncle might have gone missing fifty years ago, but that's not evidence. That's hearsay."

Per Madoc was the one to speak in reply. "You know as well as I do that the Brezhian people have been under duress these last few reigns. Many of the clans have scattered to the winds. Others see mormaers rise and fall like the seasons. Few live in proximity to the Wothwood because, as is our law, it is the primary function of the Bright Banner clan to serve as its protector and enforcer of borders. They tend to the rivers and the coastline, to the rolling hills and the plains. We, however, know different."

"And you have proof?" asked Lieutenant Shenbar, genuinely curious. Only he could manage to be accusatory and yet sound as if he were simply on the other end of a tavern table, asking questions of a traveling storyteller.

"My mother," said Mormaer Bel. "She was mormaer a time before me. Loved by her people, held up as a leader for the ages, a Champion of Fate. The Wothwood came to her in a dream, and she went into the Wothwood with her Kestenn—twelve swords—and not a single returned."

There was murmuring among the soldiers. Some were impressed, others chuckled to themselves. Judging by the look on Captain Moll's face, such an account wouldn't go terribly far.

"Professor Aoda," he said, startling her. "Come into the light a little more. I want you to meet the mormaer."

Aoda felt her heart rush to her throat and, on numb feet, she scrambled forward and put herself between the captain and Lieutenant Moll. All eyes were on her, the hounds and horses sniffing and snuffling the air around her. So many consciousnesses, so many beings, all tuned toward her. She was quite certain that, aside from her graduation at the Collegia of Yereva, there had never been so many eyes on her. She began sweating profusely in spite of the chill air, fiddling with the edging on her uniform.

Briefly, she locked eyes with the mormaer. Now, closer, she saw that Mormaer Bel was younger than she sounded. She was past marrying age, to be sure, but she still had a brightness about her than only youth carries, something she herself never possessed and always desired.

"This is Professor Aoda Kanna," said Captain Moll. "You ought to recognize her name as being Brezhian; she tells me her mother is an expatriate of one of your river clans. She, as most Brezhians in Yereva, must rely on her talents to keep her afloat in the city. And I'm told she had remarkable talents in her day."

Aoda felt tears spring to her eyes, and she blinked them back furiously. This was not the day for her to feel kinship with her mother's people. This was a day to stand strong as a citizen of Theria, a Yerevan born and bred, a symbol of the blended civilization it had become.

"Captain…" Shenbar said under his breath.

"She has spent the better part of her life learning about history and geology. Two essential components to our mission here. As such, she knows more about Brezhia than, I daresay, any of you do," Captain Moll continued, ignoring Shenbar entirely. "She understands not just the historical and mythological fabric of this island, but the literal scientific makeup. The geological makeup. The ground we stand on, right now, is unique. And speaks to the possibilities of not just a lost city full of treasure, but the resources required to bring our Empire to the very edges of the earth, to destroy the enemies that forever seek to break us down, and to alter the course of history for a thousand generations."

"Those are lofty aspirations," said Mormaer Bel, her face still unreadable, frozen a kind of aloof hardness. Aoda noticed, though, that her hand shook. The one at the reins. And her horse beneath her was beginning to tremble, as well. "And they will end in blood and death."

In the distance, Aoda thought she heard something. A flapping of wings, like a great flock descending.

The dogs heard it, too, their ears flicking back, but they remained attentive to their owners, trained as they were.

"Your story is sweet, but Professor Kanna here assures me that there is little need to be concerned. There have been no true accounts of curses, or magic, or witchcraft, in a great many years. You researched this extensively, did you not?" asked Captain Moll.

"I did," Aoda said softly. "I was part of a tribunal that sought out purported shamans and magi, many from the clans here in Brezhia. Many claiming they knew of magical woods, ponds, tributaries…"

"To the point, Kanna," said the captain.

She cleared her throat. "There is absolutely zero empirical evidence to support your claims. In all likelihood, your mother simply left. Yereva is teeming with expatriates. It is a difficult, but very likely, alternative to your story. She convinced her Kestenn to come with her, or else they did not wish for her to go alone—"

"She is not the only one to have vanished," snapped Mormaer Bel, for the first time faltering. "And I have seen it, with my own eyes. I have been to the edge of the Wothwood, seen how it doles out death in kind without thought. Seen the thousand eyes."

"Show us your proof," said Captain Moll, his hands spread as if hoping for a pittance.

Mormaer Bel straightened on her horse, raising her chin. She took a deep breath, and then just when she was about to open her mouth to say something, a voice from behind them spoke.

"I'm her proof."

It was Lon, stepping into the circle of fire. And when Mormaer Bel saw him, her face drained of all color and her eyes went wide. That rigid mask slipped for just a moment, and she looked to Aoda like a frightened little girl.

Chapter Seven
Debt

It had been seven years since he'd seen her face.

He had thought countless times about what he would do to her once he found her. All the ways he might kill her, hurt her, seek his revenge. If he would starve her or beat her, if he would chase her or feed her to a hungry bear. Or perhaps just kill her quick and burn her body. Or leave it to the carrion and watch from a distance. Or shave her head first and parade her around as his concubine and then kill her.

But then he began killing people. Professionally. And it had been so messy, so hot and difficult. Swords did not simply slide in and kill as he had heard in the tales, no matter how strong he was. There was rending and hacking, teeth flying, hair between the fingers, gasping for blood-gurgling breaths, skin slick with sweat and blood and so hard to get a hold. People, it turns out, never seemed to want to die, no matter how bad their odds of coming out on top. Many gave up every last bit of strength to fight for one more breath.

And he'd already had enough death debts to give to Sid Poole and the tyckners that imagining her death made him feel weary. She had bested him, he supposed. And as the years passed, that thirst for revenge slaked. Eventually, he hardly even thought of her when he was fighting or killing targets for Poole, and sometimes he laughed at the energy he expended thinking of doing her in so gloriously.

When he'd heard her voice in the distance, as he and Poole and a handful of others came back from their quick scouting trip up ahead, he wasn't afraid or angry. In fact, he felt tears in his eyes hearing that voice, grown deeper but no less familiar. Then he saw her, tall and bright and marvelous, a pillar of beauty and ferocity. A leader of her people, carrying kando blades like Noduuoret of old.

He was proud of her.

Speaking up was the difficult part. Stepping into that ring of horses, seeing the Kestenn gathered. It was once a dream of his to command such a group of warriors. He was jealous of her, but not in a way that was to be acted upon. He watched her, and the familiar faces before him—so many lined and grown since the last time he'd seen them—and they were somehow even stranger to him.

"I was called Braig Vann," he said, now that everyone was paying attention. Now that Glannon was watching him, saying nothing. "These days, I go by Lon."

He was no longer Braig Vann. Not really. He couldn't ask that they call him that if he hardly thought of himself that way.

Lon cleared his throat again. "There was a great hunt, seven years ago, when I was part of the Bright Banner clan."

Captain Moll looked at Lon as if he'd sprouted an extra head. He had never spoken in the man's presence, and clearly, this turn of events had surprised him. It was quite possible that Moll thought Lon entirely mute.

"You're not a tyckner?" asked the captain, disgust in every word.

"Of course he's not," Aoda said. Lon saw that she was bolstered by this sudden change of course, this emotion. Her eyes were bright beneath the squinting, and she had the look of a woman about to hit true with a sword. "Anyone could have deduced that. Put a beard on him and he's as Brezhian as wooled horses."

"As Brezhian as they come, sir," said Lon, putting a hand to his breast and bowing slightly.

"And how do you know this woman?" asked Captain Moll, his face twisted in disgust to stoop to such a low level. Lon wasn't particularly concerned that the man cared for him in any way, but if they were going to stop this madness, it was the only course of action.

Lon cleared his throat. When was the last time he had addressed anyone but Poole? It seemed strange to him that, once, he'd been trained in the oratory arts, that he'd held the chair with his father, listening to him preside over the residents of Bannercliffe from the Chair of Rule, the diadem glittering on his brow. As far deep as Braig Vann was buried, Lon had to concede that in this moment, there was at least a shard of him left. And a useful one, at that.

"I was the successor to the crown before Mormaer Bel ascended," he said, looking her in the face when he said her name. She still watched, her face as still as if she were the one left for dead. "When my father died, we went for a hunt, the entire village. There was a great beast, a boar by the looks of it, and I was intent on hunting it myself. For a time, I could see Glannon—Mormaer Bel—flanking me. She was after the same creature. I chased it far, far past where it was safe, not too far from here, in fact, where the border between the Briarwood and the Wothwood come together. The banks of the Wo River."

"And what, you were abducted by the tyckners?" asked Captain Moll, clearly ready for this story to be over.

Lon had no desire to throw his cousin before the wagons yet, and so the story he conveyed was a bit altered from his memory. "I was brash, unbelieving. Like all of you. I knew the warnings, I knew that Glannon's own mother had gone missing, that our own goddess, Noduuoret, had perished there. I knew the stories and the tales of monsters of such horror and danger, whose thirst for blood could never be quenched. But still, I persisted. I ran across the Wo River, planting my feet on the soft moss on the other side of the bank, and slayed the beast right there."

At the mention of the moss, Aoda opened her mouth to speak. No doubt she would want to know details, and they would have time to talk of it later. He held up a hand in silent plea for her to refrain from questions, and she gave him a scarred, lopsided smile.

Lon continued. "As its blood spilled across my hands and into the waters, I saw the creature change, shift. It looked to me as if black wings alighted on it, and then came a part of it. It grew and twisted, bigger and stranger. And with this new possession came a deep intelligence, a knowing. I cannot explain to you other than that I knew it was aware of me, of all my faults and my frailties, as any great enemy on the battlefield would be, even though it was dead."

They were rapt. All of them. Even the Kestenn leaned forward on their horses, taking in every word he said. Lon felt a flush of pride in himself, though he had to thank the tyckners and their long nights full of tales for the feel of it. His cadence was no longer Brezhian, and thankfully. Their stories were never so full of detail. All swords and bashed brains and battles for honor.

"And then it rose again, faster than any creature I have ever witnessed. One moment it was dead, the next I could feel its hot breath on my neck," Lon continued. "And when it came to me, I realized that my weapons were no longer of use. Though I carried with me my father's spear, one swipe past me and the great creature gouged me so deep that I fell to the ground, my spear with me."

He caught Glannon's gaze again, and she swallowed hard.

"It gored me so badly, I was certain that I would die. But I made sure it would never live again. I ripped out its tongue, I gouged out its eyes, I snapped open its maw.

"Then I sat, bleeding out into the Wothwood, ready to find my maker, knowing death would come to me before the twilight. Then, when I was prepared to cross the final river, I heard a voice…"

Pausing, Lon watched Glannon's face. She did not take her eyes off of him.

"It was Sid Poole, this man here," continued Lon, as Sid came into the circle, the contrast making him seem thinner and more angular than ever. The tattoos on his neck were a stark contrast in the dim light, fire glinting off the thousand buttons on his jacket.

There was a time when Lon was embarrassed to hold such company. But life had changed him. Understanding the tyckners had changed him, too. He knew what people saw when he looked at them, but they misunderstood these roving people. They were truly enlightened.

Poole took off his elaborate hat and bowed before the mormaer, saying softly, "Meeting you is my most sincere pleasure."

And so Lon continued, putting his hand on Poole's shoulder. "He saved my life. And so I owe him a death debt. And I will pay it, when the time comes. For now, I am sworn to the tyckners, and to their cause."

"You never went back?" asked Captain Moll, not nearly as enchanted with the story as the rest. "A big, brawny fellow like yourself—surely you could have taken this man and his people and returned to your place of power."

A good lad, a strong lad.

Father.

Lon swallowed, considering Captain Moll's words.

In that first year, there were plenty of times that Lon had considered running away. But the kindness that Poole showed him, in spite of his acerbic tongue and even sharper wit, made treachery feel vastly dishonorable. And, truth be told, the longer that he spent with the tyckners, the less he liked the man he was growing up to be. So full of ambition and greed. Always wanting something more, someone more. The tyckners didn't hold to such notions as inheritance or seats or crowns, marriages or deeds. They worked with the Empire, but it was solely a business transaction. He found a tremendous amount of value in that freedom, that detachment from the trappings of the life he'd worked so hard for in his youth.

"A big, brawny fellow might be a marvel among some of the Brezhian tribes, it true," Lon continued. "But my affairs are my own, and I have chosen to stay with the tyckners. Some oaths are stronger than others, and Fate always seems to guide us when we least expect it."

He could have said a great deal more, but he had not the need. Glannon understood his meaning, and that's all there was. For all her talk of Fate, she had clearly thought he was out of the equation entirely, that the Wothwood and the injury were enough to ensure her reign. And to some extent, it was. While he hadn't died, Braig Vann—as a concept—had.

"So what would you have us do, Lon, the tyckner guard?" asked Captain Moll, clearly unmoved by this continual drama unfolding before him. "If you were in the Wothwood and returned alive, and the tyckners were in the Wothwood and returned alive, you have done nothing to strengthen your cousin's cause here and simply made clearer inroads for me and my men."

"You misunderstand us, sir," said Sid Poole, coming into the circle of guards behind Lon.

The tall tyckner always had a habit of appearing smaller than he was, all long arms and gangly legs. But as he strode through the line of men, his wide-brimmed hat alight with the fire of a dozen torches, he seemed to unfold and lengthen, the shadows of his face making his pleasant features almost grotesque.

"Do I?" asked Captain Moll.

"You see, we are mostly in agreement. You are not alone in wishing to discover the wonders of the Wothwood; my people are a people bent on innovation, on progress. We move where the winds take us and have been rootless like seeds on the breeze for time out mind."

"You've been into the Wothwood, then?" asked Professor Aoda. She, like the rest of the company, could barely take her eyes from the tyckner. He commanded such attention it was almost as if he were a magus, enchanting them all.

Sid Poole shifted a bit, as if to gain better ground on his rootless existence. Lon always thought the man thin enough to be blown away altogether. He held a hand out, long fingers encircling something within, small and round. Another one of his buttons. Lon knew what to expect from this, understood the reasoning that this particular group of tyckners rarely left Luthland, why they were not trading in Yereva and focusing their energies on more lucrative endeavors.

"I believe Fate has indeed brought us together, to use a concept more familiar to your sort," Sid Poole said. His fingers cast shadows over the small button, like standing stones around an ancient well. "I know the Wothwood as well as any alive. We cannot take a full force, but we can go well armed. Because as the most esteemed mormaer points out, it is dangerous to tread if you don't know where to put your feet."

Glannon finally awoke from her shock and frowned down at Sid Poole. "It is our duty to protect the Wothwood—you should be flayed on the spot for trespassing in the first place, and being so blatant about your transgression."

Poole thought Glannon laughable. Lon could see it in his eyes. But though he was far outnumbered in terms of spears, he had not yet exhausted his hand. Any forward hostility would need to be saved for the wood itself.

"Mormaer, you say that your mother was lost to the Wothwood, correct?" Sid Poole asked her.

She nodded shortly, her entire body a line of impatience.

"What if I were to tell you that I have every reason to believe Noduuoret herself is at the center of the Wothwood, simply waiting for the right mormaer to free her. And that the great city lies beyond, waiting for the next great generation to claim it?"

Glannon's face was blank, but her eyes glistened. "I would say you were a charlatan, then. And a blasphemer."

"Then, let me show you something remarkable," he said.

It was then that Poole let loose the button in his showy fashion. First he tossed it in the air, letting it glint in the torchlight. Then he grabbed it midair, snapping it between his fingers, and the whole camp lit bright as day.

When they could all see again, two camulos owls had alighted on Glannon's shoulders. A black male and a white and blue female. Her house sigil.

The magic trick was enough to win the trust of the Bright Banner clan, at least for a time. Lon was not privy to discussions between Mormaer Bel, Per Madoc, and Captain Moll, Lieutenant Shenbar, and Sid Poole, but he could tell by their body language that they were making an uneasy peace. When Sid Poole returned, he was somewhat pleased with the outcome, but having had to make a few concessions—something never permitted unless absolutely necessary—uncertain about the long term.

"The lieutenant seems a good man," he said, once they had retreated to their one caravan, serving as home, camp, and travel for the small band. "But I've no trust for the captain, and he's no trust for anyone either. Having to work with the Brezhians makes his skin crawl, I can tell. Any man with that much contempt for those who look and act differently is dangerous. Once you measure others and find them wanting, you reduce them, breaking them down to the worst you see in them. As he looks up on the Bright Banner clan he sees savages, relics of a time long gone. And when he sees us, he sees but a means to achieve his goals, as we've been perceived for for centuries."

"But you think this is a chance to change that," Lon said. For most of their years together, Lon had been kept on the outskirts of all of Poole's planning. But that began to change slowly, as the tyckner realized, likely as he began to realize that Lon no longer spoke of returning home.

Poole sank into his elaborate cushioned chair, exhaling a long breath. For a moment he looked like an ancient man, one breath from death, the skin on his eyelids papery thin. But then he opened his eyes, and they burned bright with vigor and youth.

"I am like no tyckner before me," he said. "I've taken a vow to fix this Wothwood problem. I have discovered what no one else could and now stand ready to give a chance to the Brezhians, should they want it."

Lon watched him, unsure where to insert himself into the conversation—a familiar feeling when in Poole's presence. He didn't know if the man was bluffing about the city or the goddess. But the trick with the owls had been impressive.

"And you came to me, Lon. Braig Vann. Bleeding out before me, there, on the very edge of the Wothwood. A real Brezhian, ready to meet my demands and give me protection when I needed it. We've scared the piss out of half the tribes, twice over as many pirates, and made ourselves masters of this island in every way but one. Wothwood."

"I suppose that's true," said Lon.

He sighed again, shaking his head. "What do you think of all that, Lon? Does it not move you? Do you not feel part of something greater?"

"I think that I've been given a second chance at life," he said. "Or, at living, I should say. It's a different thing."

"Go on," said Poole, eyebrows up in interest.

Lon swallowed on the lump in his throat. "I'd been wondering about meeting Glannon Bel again. Or at least, I used to. But now that I've met her, I realize that I am not Braig Vann any longer. Or at least, his shadow is still upon me, but I am not made up of him, his thoughts and desires. I'm a useful tool for you, I have a purpose. I could have called her out this evening, but I did not."

"I thought that curious," said Poole. "I admit, you even had me wondering. It might have been advantageous to discredit her."

"It wasn't worth it. The Wothwood is bigger than all of us, and I agree that the tyckner cause depends on it. And there was a time that just looking at Glannon Bel made me hard enough to lose my wits. But sometime, between now and then, things have changed."

"There's Nettie in the caravan, for one," said Poole. "You'd make fine children."

"Ah, she's good. We have our fun. But when I'm done with my oath, I think I'll set sail for somewhere else. I'm not a Brezhian anymore, but I'm not a tyckner, either."

He wanted Poole to disagree with him, he realized, as he said the words. He wanted to hear that he was a tyckner, that he would always be welcome. That their paths would always cross and twine, as the old songs said.

But in that pause Sid Poole gave, Lon knew it was all a farce. Knew that the name Lon was as empty as his first name. Knew that his hope, to be accepted, was not yet realized.

"That's one of the things I wanted to speak to you about, Lon," said Poole. He opened his hands, as if in pleading or beginning a prayer. "I want to release you from your oath. I want you to go into the Wothwood of your own volition. I have strung you along on my whims for a very long time, holding you to the same standards I hold the tyckner warriors—who yes, are few but have trained their whole lives for this."

Lon felt his world tip slightly. Saw himself sprawled on the floor of the Wothwood, Glannon Bel standing over him, and wondered how the space seven years had brought him back full circle.

Chapter Eight
Revenge

THEY WERE UP BEFORE DAWN THE NEXT MORNING, PLANNING AND discussing the events as they had late into the previous night. Per Madoc was upset with Glannon on at least seven counts, but she was glad that she wasn't beyond forgiveness. She could tell that by the way he was looking at her. Angry, but not without a bit of pride. He had no idea how much seeing Braig Vann had broken her, had reduced her, had changed her. That she had been able to string together two words was nothing short of a miracle.

"I don't give a fuck what you think," she told him as he continued his angry tirade in their tent. It was an indelicate turn of phrase, but it was the truest she could give, and she had no doubt half the camp could hear her.

"You have to, by law," Per Madoc pressed.

Yuri and Caxigo were in the tent with her, and though they were attempting to keep stoic, even they were moving back and forth uncomfortably.

She was pacing, almost stomping. Glannon knew she looked like a petulant child, but she didn't care.

"I have to hold your counsel," Glannon said, knowing the decrees better than just about anyone, having had to memorize them since childhood. "I don't have to heed it."

"It's not that you kept the matter of Braig Vann secret that so concerns me, though that will take some explaining," he said. "Although Per Carro is disturbed by the events, I know it's exactly what your mother would have done."

She softened at that, inwardly. Then she said, "Fuck Braig Vann. This is bigger than him."

Per Carro, his square, severe face twisting down into his beard, was not as judgmental of her decision to go into the Wothwood. "Crass words, but I agree that her heart is in the right place. We've long known that the Wothwood could not be avoided forever. Mormaer Bel prevented an all-out occupation, something that neither we nor an entire mustered Brezhian force could have the power to prevent. And if there are riches there, and if the great city is still within our power to grasp…" His eyes glittered with the possibility.

"It's goddess bunk," Per Madoc said. "You honestly believe this drivel?"

"You have another explanation?" Per Carro said, his voice calm but his brows so low they almost eclipsed his eyes.

"For the time being, we will beg to differ on the matter of what lies within the Wothwood. I wish to speak to this surveyor, this Aoda Kanna. She's the only one around here who has a shred of sense about her," said Per Madoc. "But that begs the question about what to do with Braig Vann."

"What do you mean?" snapped Glannon.

"I don't care what you did to him, not really. It was the sign of a good mormaer. And he was a coward for not coming back to us. Still, I think you ought to speak to him," Per Madoc said. "Find out what he can tell us about the tyckners and these new strangers. Test out his mettle. Discover where his loyalties lie."

"That was a bold thing he did, still," said Per Carro, stroking his mustache thoughtfully. "Reminded me of his father. Most of the lads around his age never had the guts to do something like that. In fact, the old Braig wouldn't have, either."

"I should think that one of you speaking to him should serve well enough," Glannon said, stomach sick at the idea of sitting down, one to one. "Isn't that what you're for?"

"You owe him a great deal," stressed Per Madoc, and she could hear the double meaning in his voice. It wasn't just tonight. It was everything she'd had since the night Braig Vann had nearly bled out on the mossy ground of the Wothwood. "And before we leave the comfort of the Briarwood, in hopes to return for the first time in ten generations to the city of our making, I'd suggest you do. Before it's too late."

Per Madoc put his hand on her arm. She'd taken off her armor, and so there was nothing between them but a slip of muslin. The heat from his fingers was startling. But she did not ask him to take it away. Not with her eyes or with a command. She should have. By rights he was overstepping. But Glannon had felt his eyes on her when she'd shouted down the Therian forces. She knew what it meant.

"I'll take Yuri and Caxigo," she said with a sigh, not for the last time wondering what she had given up to become mormaer. If she could ever stop giving things up. Marrying a man like Per Madoc wouldn't have been out of the question save that he was a known Denier. And that would break her clan into pieces, wouldn't it?

So Glannon gently took Per Madoc's hand from her arm and then softly, kindly, patted the side of his cheek. His eyes widened, just slightly, and the two looked at one another.

"Be careful," she said to him, unsure why the words came, and with it a rush of an unusual emotion: a need to protect him. It was a welling ferocity.

"What do you mean, Mormaer? I can take care of myself, you know. Better than you know, I suspect," he replied, grabbing her fingers in his, not yet letting her go.

Fire, there was fire in her for him.

"Whatever happens," she said, blinking more times than she should, just to try and break eye contact with him.

Per Madoc nodded slowly, a look of confusion on his face. "As you command, my lady."

Then, heart still pounding, Glannon was out the tent flap shouting for Caxigo to get her armor again, though Yuri complained that he'd just gotten it clean.

Once she was accoutered, they set out to make their appointment. The tension in the camp was thick enough Glannon swore she could smell it. Or maybe it was just the unwashed soldiers and Therian garlic.

Bravery came naturally to Glannon Bel. Big strokes. High stakes. As long as she could recall, she was constantly poised to attack, to share a witty remark, to command with passion and strength. But now she was having a crisis of self, a meddling doubt that twisted at her as she waited for Braig Vann to come to her in the small clearing north of the camp.

She'd sent Caxigo to fetch him; the two of them had grown up together, fought together. He'd trust her. But now she was doubting the whole thing. Blaming Per Madoc for his secret meetings and scandalous smile, blaming herself for leaving Braig to die, blaming the entirety of Theria for her problems.

Maybe if she'd gone the original route, none of this would have happened. If she hadn't have listened to her mother time and again. If her mother hadn't been so obsessed with Fate. Maybe it wasn't Fate. Maybe it was the Wothwood itself, reaching out to strangle her, waiting for her. Waiting to kill her.

For a moment she felt tendrils around her heart, squeezing. Fear of the dark, fear of death, fear of everything stopping. Ceasing to be Glannon Bel. Turning back to dust and dirt. She was supposed to put her faith in Noduuoret, believe that when her death came, as mormaer, that she would be given a place at her side, in the eternal Kestenn.

Except that was even more terrifying than dying.

She shivered under her furs, gripping the braided bracelets about her gauntlets and yanking them off, throwing them to the ground. Her hands were sweating so hard they were practically chafing. She hated the feeling of gloves, anyway. Always had. And if Braig was coming armed, gauntlets were the least of her concerns.

Out of the corner of her eye, she thought she saw wings again, but then she blinked, and it was Braig Vann—Lon, as he called himself now—standing a few paces away from her, stock still. Caxigo was a few steps behind him, trying to keep from smiling.

Yuri sniffed the air. "Well, there you are, Braig," he said at last. "Cax here has always bemoaned the fact that her best sparring partner went and got himself gored to death, but now we might have to rethink that. It's good to see you."

Braig nodded and almost smiled.

Glannon watched Braig emerge and noticed immediately that he came without armor, though that didn't stop him from looking impressive. She looked for lines of familiarity in his gait and manner. But so much about him had changed. Earlier, she'd been high up on her horse, and he'd been a good distance from her. The details were hard to make out, though she'd never mistake the voice, even if it was lower than it had been. Now though, she could see all the ways that he had changed, and all the ways he had stayed the same.

His eyes were still a little dull, but they were deeper than she remembered them, lined around the edges. Most of his face was carved in ways she never imagined, having frozen him as a teenager in her mind. What was once a rather plain face was made more striking, and strangely foreign, without the beard. But there was no mistaking him, even though a thousand things had changed. The vessel remained the same. Her cousin Braig, with whom she'd shared a nursemaid and almost every day of her life until the age of fourteen.

There was no denying his size, either. When they were younger, Glannon would shield herself from his praise by saying he was only big for their village, that when he went out into the world he wouldn't be so big by comparison.

But he was still a head taller than Caxigo and considerably broader than Yuri who were both mountains among the Bright Banner clan. Thoughj he wasn't as bulky as he was during his years of training in Bannercliffe, his body had grown more lean and nimble with time. And practice. Probably a lot of that.

"Mormaer Bel," he said to her, once she let the silence go a little too long. That voice. It made her shiver. "I'm honored that you would speak with me."

No sarcasm. No irony in the tone. It sounded so damned honorable she wanted to strike him.

"I don't know what to call you," she said, willing her voice still. It worked, and she was glad of it. Her confidence returned slowly.

"Braig is fine, if you can't say Lon," he said. The word meant "boar" in the old tongue. She got the joke, twice over.

Glannon could hear Caxigo's leather creaking behind him. Given the opportunity, her money was still on Braig, though. Goddess, she had forgotten just how big he was. Even when he wasn't trying to be frightening, he was.

She remembered that night, when he was drunk and he came so close to her, and the things that he said…

"Cax. Yuri. Can you check the perimeter? I want to speak to Braig alone," Glannon said to her guards. She sounded far more certain than she felt, but then she had trained as hard in diplomacy as he had trained in combat.

The Kestenn guards nodded and departed in opposite directions. She knew that Yuri wouldn't go that far, but it was worth a shot.

When she was sure they were at least out of hearing range, she went to say something but then thought better. So it was Braig who spoke first.

"We're not far from where we first saw that boar," Braig said, taking a few steps around their meeting spot. It was a small clearing with a little fire, the dim morning light casting their bodies in hues of blue and grey.

"Are we?" Glannon asked, even though she knew well enough.

"Wouldn't you call that Fate?" asked Braig, letting out a mirthless laugh. "Your mother would."

"She would have," she said.

"You learned well from her, Glannon."

"I think so."

"Hard to believe she's been gone ten years now, isn't it?"

"No, it's not hard. I miss her every day. It never stops hurting."

Braig frowned. "I suppose that's true. You've lived with the reminders; I ran from them."

"That's an interesting perspective."

"It's the truth."

"Is Bannercliffe still the same?" he asked. "In my mind, it's preserved in amber. I hardly believed it was you on that horse, not some gawky teenager."

"Bannercliffe is the same as it always was," she replied, her voice as chilly as she could make it. "A boring town run by boring people with boring problems."

"Well, sometimes boring is good. It means you're safe."

"You call this safe?" she asked, gesturing toward the Wothwood. "You're a fool, Braig."

Braig did smile this time, scratching the back of his head as he paced. "You've changed, that's for sure. And you're right. I am a fool, and I've made peace with it. You, though. You were something else out there. Like a goddess of old. For a second I thought I'd see fire sprout from your eyes. Are those kando blades?"

"They are," she said, swallowing back a surge of pride. He was playing her, trying to sneak around the subjects, twist her emotions. She wouldn't have it.

"Fine weapons."

Enough of the banter. Glannon turned to face him, eyes narrowed as if he were her prey. "You could have turned the whole army against me last night."

He finally stopped his pacing, turning toward her to look her in the eye.

"You're not really sorry, are you?" he asked.

"I'm Mormaer Bel. I don't have time for apologies." Glannon did not let her features betray her though his words threw her. She remained as expressionless as if she had been carved into black marble. "You never contacted us, you never came back. I presumed you were dead."

"The Braig Vann you remember is dead."

"But I didn't—"

"Just because I didn't actually die doesn't mean he's not dead."

"So you've gone tyckner."

"I've adopted some of their philosophies, for certain. I've found it freeing to take life less seriously. To detach myself—"

Something moved above them. Then he froze. She froze, too. Both poised for attack, years of training springing to action before thought.

There was a sound like the chattering of a million teeth. A change in pressure, as if they'd mounted a hill too fast. Glannon's ears immediately began ringing, too, like that time she'd had a fever as a child and almost died. She could taste the sick again, smell the stink of death all around her. The fear of it sank deep into her bones before she was even aware of what was going on.

A kind of sparkling blackness pricked at the edges of her vision, and she could feel her whole body sing out in reply, fighting against the overwhelming desire she had to just fall to the ground and give up.

Braig was not well, either. She blinked over toward him, saw his mouth slack, his brows knit over his eyes. He had the wherewithal to have drawn his spear, but against what? There was nothing around them but air.

Then Yuri crashed through the trees, entwined in what looked like a silvery cloud at first. But then Glannon got a closer look: it was made up of teeth. Rows of them in an invisible mouth, moving and twisting in whorls about his head and his arms, gnashing and rolling impossibly. There was no form to it, no sense, just a madness that sent Glannon's hands trembling. Her whole body went rigid with fear and wrongness.

Yuri stumbled in toward them, swatting and grunting at the swarm, and when he saw Glannon, he opened his mouth, but it was just a myriad of tiny glittering teeth continually rearranging themselves, blood frothing with the silvery stuff.

"Yuri, fight this!" she cried, her blades up at the ready. Please, goddess, it was not worth this. She did not want to kill her friend.

But perhaps he was already dead.

Braig faltered. He blinked as if waking himself from a dream and then threw himself forward, only to come to a quick stop as Yuri fell to the ground before them, clawing at his face, his fingers raw with the effort.

The teeth were shredding him alive before their eyes, chewing his flesh from his bones with startling swiftness, sending blood spray in every direction. The sight of it, watching the man evaporate before their eyes—and leather and metal and everything else—left them both gasping and sick, unsteady on their own feet. Glannon dropped one of her blades for her hand trembled so.

They would die. They would fail.

Glannon reached out and touched Braig's shoulder because she needed to steady herself more than anything. But, to her surprise, he put his hand on hers, clasping her fingers tight. And in that touch the world became clear—brutal, but clear—and they were both flushed with a kind of warm, deep understanding. The nausea lifted. The dizziness abated.

They locked eyes, nodded. They needed to be touching, had to be. Something about that connection cut through the fear. It would mean that Glannon would have to fight with her off hand, but she'd trained enough to know her way around fairly well; you couldn't master the art of kando blades without knowing how.

Looking over at the swarm, Glannon noticed the pattern now. It was like a flower, coming down from a narrow passageway above and then blooming out. At the very edge, there was a source, if it could be called that. A concentration point.

Forward they moved, without speaking, Braig holding aloft his sword more like one might a shield, protectively.

Glannon felt a growing warmth where their hands met, a kind of pulsing that wasn't altogether distressing. It was as if there was something else tying them together besides their own strength.

Getting her feet under her was a little more difficult than she would have hoped, but given the circumstances, she was quite relieved.

"Don't let go," she said to Braig, and he nodded curtly as if he'd already made that connection ten times over. "Whatever you do."

"Is that a request?" he said through a tight jaw.

"It's an order."

They moved as one toward the swarm, both looking for an opening in the churning madness, hoping they could find an advantage.

But then the game changed again.

The silver streams of sharp fragments rose, twisted, and then entered Yuri through his nostrils, mouth, ears, and eyes. For a moment his skull was lit so bright his skin glowed like candle wax below a flame.

A buzzing sound began, rattling Glannon's mail. She shuddered against it, moving back a step with Braig in tow.

Then Yuri rose. The borders of his body swelled as the swarm filled him, his leather jerkin puffing up and spilling out of his collar, his shoulders rising, his head gaining mass like a boil ready to burst.

Yuri. Her friend. A face she had known since they played together Old Ruse's herb house, raised along with her to be her guard and her protector.

Now, this. Whatever this was. Glannon knew without question that he was dead, he was gone, and that this body before her, growing sickeningly large before her eyes, was not him.

It was her duty to destroy him. As mormaer of the Bright Banner, as her mother before her. She was the flame in the dark.

So as the creature that was Yuri rose, his two-sided axe along with him, Glannon didn't hesitate. She had enough of a warrior's instinct to close the chamber of her heart where Yuri had been, to seal away a lifetime of memories and feelings, and attack.

Braig twisted to the side and dropped his spear, on purpose, reclaiming the shield Yuri had dropped. It was a better option, and she gave him the slightest of nods.

In this way, they could have more cover as they approached the beast.

Like a strange turtle they moved forward, Braig at the fore, holding up the shield and buffeting the stray teeth that clattered toward them as if pulled by an invisible force. They plinked off like hail.

The kando blade was long enough, and the angle just manageable enough, that Glannon could strike out when needed.

It wasn't hard to find a good opening. The creature that inhabited Yuri's body was clumsy, unaccustomed to such confines. But slashing through its arm, even with excellent aim considering the poor positioning, was like cutting through sand. It just reformed again, the cloth and skin falling off it in ragged slices.

"Going to need to rethink this approach," breathed Braig, so close to her ear it tickled. They were both getting tired, and even though their hands had grown slick with sweat, neither had loosened their grip.

He was going to say something more, but Glannon swung around and aimed to take a good chunk off the side of the creature's head. The attack was true, but again, it made almost no impact. She felt a shudder run through her as the teeth scraped against her blade, vibrating all the way up her arm and setting her jaw against it.

That reaction was enough to ruin their flow, however. A big, studded fist caught her in the chin, sending her back, crashing over Braig. Her foot caught, twisting her ankle and making it crunch, and her elbow hit his nose with an equally brittle response. Their hands flew apart, and they both landed on their backs.

Both were up in mere moments, but they were lost to horror now. The sound of it, that was even worse than the appearance. And the smell, too. Somehow, with their hands together, they had avoided those two senses. But now Glannon felt an unbearable urge to vomit, her hands trembling so much that she doubted she could manage another blow. At least her other blade was nearby. She scrambled to grab it.

Braig charged forward, wobbling on his legs like he was drunk. He had nothing but the shield he was carrying, and he used this to buffet the blows from the creature as he tried to kick its legs out from under him. But it might as well have been made of smoke for all the good it did.

Up went one of Yuri's swollen arms, chunks of flesh evaporating as the continued roiling of shards churned beneath the remnants of his clothing, and then down on Braig's back. Glannon hissed sharply seeing how quickly that blow sent him to the ground. That huge man, that trained and dangerous man, flat on the ground, blood pooling around his chin.

She shook her head, hoping to dispel some of that incessant whining sound—it did not work—and then charged forward, both kando blades in her trembling hands, her feet pumping furiously to mark the space between them and prevent a killing blow to Braig, if he wasn't finished already.

Before she even reached the creature, it had coiled around her, one arm snaking out like a tentacle, wrapping around her waist and squeezing her tight. Cutting through her mail, slipping under her armor, slicing through to her skin. She would be cut in half, she knew it. Sliced as perfectly as a presented boar for a feast day. And she hadn't even set foot in the Wothwood yet.

Hearing a crunch behind her, Glannon shouted as she felt her sides searing with pain anew, preparing to die and hoping against all else that there was a miracle somewhere nearby.

And there was.

It came in the form of four people: Caxigo, Sid Poole, Professor Aoda Kanna, and Lieutenant Shenbar.

There was a blue flash, like Glannon had seen during her proclamation, and something flew toward the abomination. It was no human form, nothing that remotely could be mistaken for anything living. But it did have a kind of lively essence, a force of heat and movement.

At first her eyes were blinded, but she did not lose her footing. Enough to rattle her, sure, but Glannon had spent her lifetime training for battles—granted, none like this—and she refused to bow to fear of the unknown in front of everyone.

The light entered what was left of Yuri, and as soon as it made contact, Glannon felt her breath return and the pressure at her sides relent. Death would not come yet, though the whole world sang of it. Reeked of it. Bled for it.

The creature that was once her most trusted guard stumbled backward, the teeth frozen in midair and unable to resume their frantic dance. The entire form ceased to move, all the edges of it pulsing with a counterpoint of light—not blue but eldritch yellow—as if pushing an invisible boundary and meeting resistance. Glannon didn't understand how she felt it, but she knew there was a battle going on.

Taking the moment to reset her stance, she caught Braig's eyes as he slowly rose, his heavy shoulders like a mountain waking from an eternal slumber. The yellow reflected in his eyes, his bared teeth. He did not look her way. There was something inside of him, something that made her afraid for the first time.

But then came a buzzing sound from deep within the creature that was once Yuri, like millions of cicadas beating their wings at once coupled with a high-pitched whine.

Then…

Nothing.

It just dropped.

All the fragments of teeth fell to the ground, smoking and evaporating before Glannon could get to them. Yuri's body was reduced nothing but shredded armor.

"Noduuoret," she whispered. "Save us."

Chapter Nine
Value

Aoda Kanna could not reconcile what she had just seen with the logic of her education. She had known that magic existed on some level, but its presence was far diluted from the days of yore, and she had come to believe that it was all easily explained with science or psychology. People wanted to believe they were healed, and they felt better. Flames changed color, of course, but all one needed to know was the right components to add to the fire. Prophecies came true? Well, there were entire fleets of Elutil devoted to writing and interpreting prophecies. Certainly some of them would prove true eventually.

But what she had just seen. That creature. The one that had taken over the body of the Brezhian guard and shredded him, nearly destroyed Lon and the mormaer.

That abomination had wanted to kill them. Would have. Almost did. Even now one of the healers was examining the mormaer; her armor had been sliced down to her skin, and she required stitches, a thousand tiny abrasions in her skin as if she'd run through a house of glass.

And Lon. Aoda could scarcely believe the state he had been in, reduced to a shaking, quivering lump of a man. Even now he had a haunted look in his eyes and took longer to answer questions every time someone asked.

Shenbar had wanted a full report on the matter, even though he was sure that Captain Moll wasn't going to believe a word of it. Theirs was a small group dispatched from the main camp to investigate the strange noises coming from the direction of where they'd found the mormaer and the tyckner guard. They'd met up with the one called Caxigo right before things got really ugly.

After she'd interviewed Lon and given him some strong liquor from the flask she kept with her, she had to return to the captain herself with her findings. She'd written everything down precisely as possible and presented them in person in his tent.

"I can't share this with Yereva," Captain Moll said, throwing the paper down on the crate that served as his desk in the tent. "Professor Kanna, I appreciate the skill with which this is written, but you're here to be the analytical mind among us. You're here to measure science up against the beliefs of these rather barbarous individuals."

She felt her face flush hot, anger flaring. "I'm telling you, Captain, there is no scientific explanation for what I saw. It had sentience. It had purpose. I could have explained countless different occurrences, but nothing with that much clear malice and intent." She paused, noting the way he'd phrased the question. "Didn't you see it?"

"There wasn't much left to see by the time I arrived," he said.

"Lon was afraid. The mormaer was, too."

"Barbarians, Kanna. You can't tell me you're starting to believe their babble?"

"I'm only saying it's beyond explanation. And dangerous, no matter what way you look at it."

"This is a strange place, I will give you that. But I'm more likely to attribute this to swamp gas. Or, perhaps, a swarm of wasps. It's been known to happen."

Aoda chewed on her bottom lip. Of course she'd thought of those things. "I don't know what you want me to do, then. I cannot in good conscience say that we have enough evidence to make a safe trip into the Wothwood with our forces. There is too much risk for loss of life."

The captain sighed at her, making her feel so much less for having let her fear seep through. But it was there, all around her, pressing in on her skin and in her ears. As if the pressure in the place was all wrong.

"Listen. Professor. Because of your work, I know we're sitting near a geological crossroads. If my sources are correct, we are near iron stores of the likes no one has seen in millennia. Copper, too, perhaps. Rare as anything, and in quantity never seen anywhere in the Empire. You believe, as I do, that the Brezhians have simply made this elaborate myth—and perhaps managed a rather theatrical diversion to convince you otherwise."

"But why would they have bothered to present themselves to Lon and to the mormaer?" she asked, finding her courage even if just a little. She swallowed on a dry mouth, wishing she hadn't given so much of that liquor to Lon. But he needed it more than she did. "They're not the ones who need to be scared off. We are."

"That's what you must find out."

"It's too dangerous to march the whole of our force through the wood in one go like this," she pressed. "I won't allow it. I could never live with myself."

Captain Moll raised a single, perfect eyebrow. Gods, but the man was beautiful. She hated herself for thinking that, hated herself for being so damned easy to charm. He was a monster, she knew that. If he had his way, the entirety of the Wothwood would be reduced to nothing but cinders, all to make it easy enough to rape the earth of its precious ore. And her work had drawn them here. Her taking samples from the other islands, from the ocean floor, reading maps and histories and putting together the puzzle. She was as complicit in this as he was.

And she would be paid handsomely when it was all over. Enough for a new life, not just for herself, but for her mother as well. Enough to move out of the hovel she'd called home when she wasn't at the Collegia, to begin her real work and research.

Captain Moll pushed himself slowly up from his chair, leaning forward. He looked her straight in the eye, and she could not look away even if a creature like the one who'd killed Yuri was standing over her shoulder.

"If that is what you truly believe, then I order you to take a small group ahead of us. Your choice. A dozen, perhaps. Scout for us and come back with the report, and then we shall proceed," he said. "Poole seems eager enough."

"But sir, I'm not equipped—"

"Orders, Kanna. Surely you've lived among soldiers long enough to know what that means."

When she was a child, Aoda used to dream of finding a new face. The dream took shape almost the same way every time. She was lost in a wood of birch trees, their stark white trunks like ghosts around her, their bark slashed with black lines like striped cats. She would walk through, examining each tree trunk until she found one with a face on it. It was never the most beautiful face, not like the women who lived in the brothel with her mother, but it was finely made. No scarring, no lumps. Bright eyes and a strong mouth. She reached out and peeled the face from the wall of the tree and, before it even had let go entirely, it fluttered to her own face like butterfly wings.

In the dream, she knew it was just a mask. But it was a mask she was willing to wear every day of her life.

She wished people could see past the face she had; she wished people knew how well she knew their thoughts as they looked at her.

Except maybe Lieutenant Shenbar. When he found her, she had been crying, and that made her face look even worse. Mottled and uneven, pink and pale in all the wrong places. But he didn't seem to care. He never had.

"There's no shame in being afraid," he told her, putting his arm around her as they walked together on the edge of the camp. "And you're certainly far from the first. I've seen soldiers cry on their first day with the captain, and this is the first time I've ever seen him get to you."

"But I'm not a soldier," said Aoda, pointing out the obvious. "And he doesn't understand. We should abandon this effort, go back home, and get more instruments—more men and knowledge and tools—and then approach it. He's just sending us into slaughter."

"Not necessarily," said a third voice.

Sid Poole was in the shadows, as he almost always tended to be. Aoda had not had much time to speak to him directly, usually sending messages through Lon. But now that Lon was recovering, Poole was without his guard and, apparently, up to casually eavesdropping whenever the fancy struck.

Tyckners were perilously difficult to understand sometimes.

Shenbar stiffened and removed his arm from around Aoda, looking oddly guilty about it. She missed the feeling of his warmth immediately, but his smell lingered about her still. Bright, citrusy.

"Is that right?" asked Shenbar of the tyckner. "Although your little flash bombs have been rather impressive, I'm not sure that we can attack an entire forest with them."

Poole grinned, tossing up one of his little buttons and catching it again in his hand. "Oh, that's not what I'm suggesting. Though these are most certainly helpful, I'm of a mind that if we approach the wood in the right way, in the respectful way—the intelligent way, mind you—with a smaller force, which it seems Professor Kanna has already secured, then we may have a chance."

"And you're the intelligent way, I presume," said Shenbar before Aoda could say something a little less combative and a bit more welcoming to conversation. For all that she admired Shenbar, he did not seem to have any patience with the tyckners, not even Poole. "I'd not advise taking someone like him, Aoda."

"I am the experienced way, if you should choose," Poole said. "There is more to the story of Lon and the mormaer, and I have not shared it with anyone. I can take a small group through the Wothwood, to survey and to do what you wish… but we have mutual interests."

"We get access to resources, you get the acknowledgement, and the mormaer gets to pass through the Wothwood unscathed, cementing her leadership to the Bright Banner clan and, perhaps, all of Brezhia," Aoda said, the words falling quickly into place. "And you're the key to all of that."

Poole looked at her, pleased. "That would be the way of it. You catch on quickly, Professor. It's one of the reasons I like you. But you haven't told me the entire story of why you're here."

She wasn't sure what to make of that. Being liked by a tyckner was never high on her list, but the truth?

"Lieutenant?" she asked.

"Tell him about your research," he said. "We owe him that much, at least. Given these challenges. And it isn't as if the tyckners have any loyalty to the Brezhians, anyway."

She took a deep breath. "I studied the geology here. There are indications of… well, a kind of convergence since the Vanishment," she pressed. "Striations. It leads me to believe that there was some great, cataclysmic event that, using a tremendous amount of magnetism, managed to siphon or draw all the metals toward a singular place. And if that's the case, then it's tremendously dangerous, which would serve to reason that it's protected, at least that's about what I can figure what happened last night. I can't seem to explain it."

"Can't you?" asked Poole. "It has all the markings of the supernatural from what I could see."

Shenbar frowned. "I don't think she's talking about what we saw last night. She means in terms of science."

"What is magic other than science waiting to be explained?" the tyckner drawled, rolling his eyes. "But, she is correct. There are places we must seek out. Especially the center."

"But that's where the city is," said Aoda. "The great Brezhian capital of yore. That's what the mormaer wants."

"Is it?" Poole asked, flipping the button in his hands again. Up and down. Aoda couldn't help but look at it. That he would handle metal so casually was enough to have him mugged in Yereva, no questions asked. "Or is it what you want? What you would have taken, whether or not I came to help?"

Shenbar looked cowed, clearing his throat. "What are you accusing us of, exactly?"

"Exactly what I implied. I am not an imbecile, though I sometimes play the part. The makeup of your force? The sanctioned research? You'd have gone through and taken it, without my help, and conveniently, too. It would have been a good ruse to rekindle the war with the Brezhians, one they could never win due to their own terribly splintered forces," Poole said. He spoke so matter of factly, so effortlessly. "Which, of course, has been ushered along with help from Yereva itself. Planting spies, moving the needle, just like Per Madoc over there." He pointed toward where the per was speaking with his mormaer.

Aoda had suspected the man was far keener to the details of their adventure, but that he knew more than she did made her blood run cold. She hadn't stopped to think about the kinds of soldiers in their force, but now she realized just how blind she has been. Shenbar was the only peacekeeper, when she knew full well that the Therian army had plenty to spare. There were seasoned soldiers among their ranks, built for following orders, not brokering peace.

How had she missed it? So absorbed in the details, in her own work. In Captain Moll.

Poole kept speaking, too, as her failure sunk in. "And to say nothing of the force waiting on the other side of the island. An uneasy alliance with the pirate fleet, I suppose, isn't worth losing this much wealth. Even if Aoda's calculations are within a fifty percent margin of error, you will have ore beyond your wildest dreams."

"Lieutenant," Aoda said, her voice barely above a whisper, focusing on the issue of Shenbar's honesty rather than her own shortcoming. "Is this true?"

"It's not… entirely untrue," Shenbar tried, his face contorting but unable to meet Aoda's eyes. "But it hasn't been of my own devising. My orders come from much higher, you have to understand—"

Her anger was cold, so cold. She felt as if she was going to freeze to death from it, rattling her nerves and setting her ragged teeth. Breathing wasn't a problem so much as remembering not to breathe so fast.

All her work. All that support she'd received. All the diplomacy and working with the tribes. It had all been a ruse. For what? To bring the tyckners to protect them? To allow the politicians to say they had tried everything to prevent a war? To commit genocide?

It didn't make a difference that Shenbar had been ordered because he'd lied to her. To her face. Day in and day out. He'd never once had the respect to take her aside and clue her into the farce, spare her the embarrassment. How sincere she must have looked! It was bad enough she knew there was an ulterior motive, but to find that that was just the beginning?

"You have to understand, if your calculations are true..." tried the lieutenant. "The benefit to the Empire..."

She took a deep breath, holding up her hand and turning to the tyckner. "Enough. I accept your terms, Poole. I do so as the representative of Captain Adamen Moll of the 31st regiment of his Lord Re's army in Brezhia. I will deliver a list of names shortly to number twelve."

"Aoda..." Shenbar said, his voice painfully pleading. "Let me explain."

She glared at him, as best as she could with her pitiably small, squinty eyes. "Oh, I hope you're shredded by a tooth monster!" she shouted at Shenbar, then turned away.

Nothing made any sense.

Nothing made sense.

Nothing. No. Thing.

Why didn't it just make sense? Like it was supposed to?

During her studies when something didn't adhere to logic, she could always find a book or a scroll that, eventually, shed light on the situation.

Not here. Out here near the Wothwood, Aoda felt like a ship without a compass. All her abilities were eroding away. She was alone, more alone than she had ever been before. And all those thoughts of friendship! What an imbecile she was.

That buzzing, the one that had begun when she had seen the monster trying to destroy Lon, it hadn't stopped. It was pressing at her, making her eardrums rattle as she pored over the names on the list she was putting together for the captain. In spite of the chill, droplets of sweat fell from her brow to the parchment, and she kept smudging the ink.

She was deep in it now, there was no denying. Complicit because she didn't know better, because she didn't ask enough. Because she'd spent so much time daydreaming after Captain Moll, she'd forgotten that Ori Shenbar was his right hand man, that he was a soldier first, and never a friend.

Who needed friends? She didn't.

Initially she had considered leaving Shenbar off the list. She didn't want him near her, not after the betrayal. And she had enough presence of mind to recognize at least a little ulterior motive. No, she didn't want him dead. But he was a relatively known quantity. And Aoda couldn't argue he had skills.

Not Shenbar.

But he…

No. Can't.

Yet…

As she penned the names on the parchment paper, each nib scratch sharper than the next in her ears, she found that no matter how many times she rewrote the list, Shenbar's name was always on top.

And Lon. And Glannon Bel. Her guard, Caxigo. One of those pers, she'd let Glannon choose. And Aoda's own name, the ink blotting unhappily around the characters that shaped her name. Plus a handful of soldiers she knew more by reputation than name. Kasak, Menah, and those two others who favored pikes. At least they were waiting for bloodshed.

She fussed with the list once again, trying on a new sheaf. Couldn't look untidy, not for the captain. Once she submitted the list, there would be no going back. With Captain Moll's seal, which had been waiting on her makeshift desk like an invitation, they would not be able to refuse or else suffer the penalty of treason, death. All of them, even the Brezhians, were technically Therian citizens, even if they hated it.

Never had her hand wielded such power, and she wished that she did so with a more even temper. But her small world felt crowded and full of fear, and there was no time for such thoughts.

Someone was in the doorway.

"Would you permit me within, Professor Kanna?"

Lon.

She wanted to say no, but there was such a note of kindness to his voice and a sharp weariness that she couldn't turn him away. Her mother never could turn men away, either. That was part of what ended her in so much trouble in the first place.

"Come in," Aoda said, not looking up.

He darkened the room with his form, filling the small space with heat and the scent of sweat. Fire, too.

"I'm coming with you," he said.

"Good, I already wrote your name down," she said, pointing to it with the feather side of her quill. "So that's settled."

He took a long pause, measuring her.

"I'm sorry," she said, unable to let her anger linger. She dropped the pen, sank her head into the palm of her hand. What was she thinking, speaking to Lon that way? Speaking to anyone that way? She was sending him to uncertain doom, and for one mad moment, she was actually pleased about the whole business.

"It's been a stressful day for everyone," Lon said, evenly. He walked two steps to her right and grabbed a stool, the only other piece of furniture in her tent beside the bedroll and the rickety desk, and sat on it. It creaked beneath his weight.

"No, that was inexcusable. That's no way to speak to someone," Aoda muttered.

"Captain Moll does it all the time."

"Yes, but he's Thrice Blessed by the Elutil. He is cleansed of sin and strife," she muttered, sarcasm dripping as thick as she could spread it. "And he's a colossal arse tick."

"Arse tick?" Lon asked, quirking an eyebrow.

"They're more common toward the Sands," she explained. "Little bugs. They tend to enjoy warm, moist crevices. They cling there like barnacles full of blood until they pop." Aoda twisted her hands as if strangling an invisible chicken to death.

Lon blinked at her. "You really are in a mood."

"And I shouldn't be. *You* should be. But here you are, calm as a newly fed calf glutted on mother's milk."

"I want to ask you about what happened today," he said to her, his voice gone surprisingly low, cutting through the convivial moment they'd shared.

Aoda swallowed. She didn't want to talk about that. She didn't want to acknowledge that something so outside of her learning had happened, had challenged her, and now led her to have to make such a terrible choice. And to feel so very unhinged.

Something outside snapped. A twig, probably. Just someone walking by. But she flinched anyway.

Lon, bless him, didn't make mention.

So she cleared her throat and spoke.

"I'm afraid I don't have much to say other than… it defies all my learning. Everything," she said. "And in all of that, in the face of such a damned monstrosity, both Poole and Moll are using it to their advantages. And I'm just a stupid little pawn who played right into their hands. To say nothing of your mormaer."

"She's decidedly not that," he replied. "But you're right. We are being pulled by strings. You and I, especially. It seems we've both been following men who are planning circles around us."

"You heard about that?"

"Poole told me," he said. "I'm sorry," Lon said, looking down at his hands. They were covered in little bites.

Those teeth. That man.

Aoda shuddered.

"You have nothing to be sorry about, Lon. Of all the arse ticks here in the camp, you're far from the first that should be seeking forgiveness."

He shook his head, looking so like a child. A frightened child. So strange in that immense body of his.

"It's not the whole story, what I told everyone," he said. "And I don't know why I should be telling you except that… you seem more like me than anyone else here."

Aoda tried not to feel flattered. People, as a rule, didn't approach her with feelings of camaraderie. And if you'd lined up the entire camp side by side, there was perhaps none as unlike her as Lon, tyckner or not. He might have been twice her size if she crouched just a little bit.

"I hardly think that's true, but go on," she said.

He sighed like the bellows, his big shoulders rising and falling. "Before I became Lon. When I was Braig. I wasn't a very good person. I was ambitious and conniving. I was arrogant and full of pride. The night I was gored…"

"The mormaer. She was with you, wasn't she?" Aoda asked. She'd guessed as much, and Poole had said their story was known to him, and more complex. Besides, there was something in Glannon Bel's face that didn't figure right while Lon told his story the night before. "Or something to that effect. The details of your story were a little too well knit together for my tastes."

"She found me. Bleeding to death. And she left me to die," he said, closing his eyes. "Just walked away."

There was no fury in his face. No tension in his stance. Lon breathed evenly and composedly, stating the facts without malice or anger. Which was far from what Aoda felt. The admission brought her to her feet, knocking over one of the ink pots and spilling over two of her scratched out lists. Didn't matter anyway, but that wasn't the point.

"And you let her go? You lied for her? In front of *everyone*?"

"Keep your voice down, Professor Kanna, please. This is not your anger to bear."

She sat down slowly, smoothing the front of her shirt as if being less wrinkled would prevent her from feeling so furious over the matter. It was one thing to surmise that they had been hunting the boar together, but another that she had walked away from her dying cousin.

"I don't know why you're telling me this," Aoda said. "I've got some big decisions to make tonight, and I'm very tired. And if you don't want me to be angry for you, well, I don't have anything else to offer. I'm out of pity at this point."

"I hated her for a long time, Aoda." He used her first name only this time, gentle. "But that hate… it faded. I know why she left me like that."

"Pride? Ambition? All those other, undesirables you mentioned before?"

"I'd hurt her. I'd never been kind to her when I should have been. I didn't respect her. Not her mind and not her body. One thing I've learned living among the tyckners is that the Brezhians are truly lacking when it comes to the way they train their men, in the way they allow their men to behave, especially if they're bound for power. If a woman isn't in line for mormaer or a Kestenn, she's considered free game."

"Yes, but you're not like that now."

"No, but I was. You'd have hated me."

"I doubt that."

"Still. I can't imagine what Glannon's had to endure as mormaer—and I bet half the reason she's treated so well is out of respect for her mother. And because, well, I think her mother would have done the same thing if given the chance. We Brezhians are a brutal people, and maybe the Wothwood makes us so, or maybe we use it as an excuse, but it's true. I've seen more of this world than I ever bargained for, and we're among some of the biggest arse ticks."

She almost smiled, but his admission did make Aoda consider for a moment. A man the size of Lon, even younger, more brash. He had never threatened her before, and men were generally more revolted by her then pressed to grope at her. But it's not that it had never happened before. As her mother had told her, everyone is at the end of someone's appetite.

He continued when Aoda fell silent. All the words she'd had a moment ago had flitted out of reach, so it was just as well. Suddenly there was a gulf between them.

"I wanted to tell her, to acknowledge what she'd done. I wanted her to say that she was sorry, that she regretted it. I don't know why. Maybe because I'd forgiven her, I hoped... but then that thing came at us and... it's a blur. She's hurt much more than I am, being tended to by the healers, and I think maybe..." He looked down at his hand, at the little red flecks against his skin. "Maybe we broke something, together, some part of the Wothwood. I broke the rule, first. I woke the Wothwood. Maybe she pushed me toward the border, but I went. I went because I was proud and cocksure, and now... Yuri... we grew up together, fought... together... to see... someone torn up... like that..."

The sobs came softly at first, so subtle that Aoda first thought he was just catching his breath. But then his whole body quaked with it.

Before she could stop herself, she was around the table, doing her best to comfort him. Or, at least attempting to. She could no better embrace a Brezhian fir.

Sometimes, her mother had told her, *a man doesn't want to be between your legs. I've stayed entire night with men of remarkably high repute, men who spend their coin as if I would do the most wicked tricks of the trade... who simply want to talk. To be heard. To be held. To hold me. To be reminded of something so simple, so basic, so beaten out of them. And it is in me to give that comfort, even if my heart is absent from it. It's no different than any other act in that way.*

Except for Aoda, she was not absent from it. Not at all. Her heart burned for him—not out of desire, but of that aching love one has for another soul lost to grief and pain, and knowing what it feels like in your bones.

Chapter Ten
Names

His name.

Not his name.

His father. Not his father. Someone else. A Therian. He'd not believed the words when Glannon had told him, all those years ago. But then Aoda saw through him. Through those hideous, spectacled eyes.

He didn't want to believe her. But he knew that she saw things. Had to. It's the only way she could get by in life, what with a face like that. And that mind. The way she understood things, saw patterns and designs, always had a logical reason for everything. But she was afraid, too.

As he left her tent, not caring what the soldiers whispered as he walked by, he knew the names on the list. He knew where they were going and what it meant. And it all hinged on the power of one man.

Sid Poole. And Lon wasn't certain that he could avoid punching the man in the face the next time he saw him. He and Moll should be the only ones allowed to go into the Wothwood, if not for the small chance that they'd inherit the treasure of a lifetime.

Except that was not who interrupted him.

"Lon—do you have a moment?" asked a voice. Lieutenant Shenbar. The sycophant of that horrid Captain Moll.

He hesitated, wondering. Was this what his father had been like? No, likely not. Probably just some rabble, a disgusting man with a gritty pike in his hands. Just like he had once been. Set on wetting his cock any chance he could get. Not worried about the consequence. Thinking that the women wanted it. And some of them did, and some of them wanted him. He just always wanted the ones he couldn't get.

"I'm sorry about what happened," the lieutenant continued, taking a step back.

"*You're* sorry?" All the wrong people were apologizing today.

"I've seen men die, too. I know…"

"You've seen men turned to froth and dust by a million sharp teeth, have you? Men you've known since childhood reduced to gurgling blood and slips of skin?"

Lon felt the bitterness wrap around him like armor. It might be brittle, but he'd hold onto it now.

Shenbar didn't look upset though. He simply nodded and said, "You're right. I deserve that. No one here understands any of this. Except maybe Sid Poole. And even then, who's to say?"

"Worth the gamble for all that ore though," Lon pointed out, trying to move past the Therian but finding the way blocked. Too many horses in the way. Too much movement. Why were there so many people? Why were they all moving so much? Why was it all so damned bright?

"Spoke with Aoda, I see," Shenbar said, now looking embarrassed. He sighed heavily. "Well, as I told her, I'm happy to represent Theria in the scouting party. I accept that this may be a futile effort, and we'll perish, but I could imagine worse fates. There were rumors of another plague coming through Yereva…"

"We'll be lucky if we just perish," Lon said. "By the time the Wothwood's done with you, you'll be praying for the kindness of a plague."

Lon found Per Madoc and Caxigo holding court outside Glannon's tent. He didn't know why he went that way, to her, because the last time they tried to talk, it hadn't gone so well. He'd gotten his words all wrong, studded them with anger, regret.

But for all his meandering, there was the truth of what happened when they'd touched. When they'd held hands. They were stronger. Together. Something, someone more. There was no lore to this effect that he could recall, though Lon had to admit he wasn't always paying attention during his studies as a child. If anyone had answers, it was Glannon Bel.

Still, she had fought for his life. Poole might have truly saved them, but she would have died for him, he knew that, in that moment. No one had every fought like that for him before.

Regardless of what had happened with Yuri, he couldn't shake that new knowledge. That squirming, strange sensation as their skin met. He had to talk to her about it, even if the timing wasn't ideal. It never was, really. And soon it would be too late.

"Braig, I know you're disoriented and upset, but she's not seeing anyone right now," Per Madoc said, cool and calm.

"Don't call me that," Lon replied.

"It's the name you were given on your first moon," Per Madoc replied. "It's the name Noduuoret blessed you with."

Lon spat on the ground. "As if you care a tyckner's fart about what Noduuoret blessed anyone with. I want to talk to Glannon."

"The mormaer is not taking guests. She's not feeling well," Per Madoc reiterated.

Lon remembered Per Madoc, before. A sly fellow then, a sly fellow now. There had been talk that he'd be an emissary to Yereva, even when they were young. Madoc was only a few years older than he was, but he carried those extra years as if they bestowed him with greater power. He always had. Now, older, he hadn't lost that air. The women had always said he was handsome, and Lon could see that clear enough. But there was a craftiness there that he didn't like.

But Lon was bigger than Per Madoc. Much bigger. And he didn't care about rules that protected the pers from danger because, hells, he wasn't a Brezhian anymore. Lon wasn't the right name, but it was the one he'd chosen for himself. He'd keep it until he found a better one.

"I know she's not fucking feeling well," Lon said, moving forward, casting his shadow over Per Madoc. "Did you not notice that I was right fucking there with her?"

Lon watched Per Madoc squirm, heard Caxigo go for her weapons, think twice, then grip her sword.

"I don't want to see any more blood today, Per Madoc," Lon finally said, the effort to keep from shouting it making his jaw ache.

"You don't have to," came a voice from within. Glannon. "Unless you want a peek at my side, but I think it'd swear you off women for a lifetime." Her face, lovely but pale, emerged as she pulled aside the tent flap, gripping her side with her other hand. Dried blood had crusted under her nose, and her eyes were both bruised.

Looking at her that way, he remembered then what had driven him so mad all those years. He didn't just want her, though that had always been first and foremost in his mind. He'd loved her, too. Loved her because she embodied every strength he lacked. Composure. Even temper. Wit. Endurance. She'd always had to fight harder for everything, and that made her remarkable.

Even now, thinking of her actions at the edge of the Wothwood made him see how hard of a choice that had been, but how merciless she was about it.

She made a better mormaer than he would have ever been. Maybe she wasn't a good person anymore, not in the way that someone like Sid Poole might have measured her. Honor wasn't part of it. But duty, cleverness. That had to count for something.

For the first time, Lon actually hoped that the Wothwood wouldn't kill them all.

She and Madoc would make a good pair someday. They would have handsome, strong children. Lon saw the vision of the two of them so bright in his mind that he had to shake his head to find himself in the present again.

What was happening to him?

"I think… that Lon is a bit tired from the events of the day," Glannon said, stressing his new name and looking pointedly at Per Madoc. "I'm well enough to entertain a relative."

She had heard everything.

Of course she had.

"I'm pretty sure we're just going to die," Glannon said as soon as she drew the tent flap shut with a snap. "It's the most obvious outcome."

Lon watched her gather herself, sitting down on the cot that the Therians had made for her. A woman of this rank, they figured, needed a little more than a litter on the floor. For his part, he'd just been sleeping in a hammock outside the caravan.

She still didn't look well. But that was to be expected, given what she'd endured. He was battered and bruised, a big scab itching at his chin, but he'd not had the brunt of it. It was far from the first time someone had clocked him in the head. Granted, the first time it was from a monster made of a million teeth, but still.

They hadn't tried to saw him in half.

"How do you feel?" he asked.

Lon felt like he had to keep a good distance from her across the room. He was compelled to touch her again, the thought consuming the better part of his brain for a few breaths before she spoke.

Her back was turned to him, and she wasn't wearing her armor. The roughspun she wore was speckled with blood in a stripe across her back and over to her stomach.

"I've felt better," she said. "But that's not really relevant to our current troubles, is it?"

"The word is that we leave at daybreak," he told her, knowing that she'd already have that information but not wishing to sound surprised by the tactics. "We're both on the list. But I think you should reconsider, given what happened last night."

"I'm perfectly capable," she replied. "And I'll have my people with me."

"Per Madoc?" asked Braig.

Glannon almost smiled, then stopped as if thinking better of it. "Per Carro. Per Madoc needs to stay here as my proxy. In case something happens. In case I'm…" She trailed off, looking for the right words. "In case we don't come back."

"You think it's worth dying for?"

Glannon's shoulders rose and fell, but she didn't answer. She pushed her braid over her shoulder so it cut a neat line down her back. All those movements she made. He knew them. She had changed, in ways one would expect with age, but she was still the same Glannon he had pined over—and been brutal to—for years.

It was driving him crazy, to want something—again—that he couldn't have. Or shouldn't have.

But when she spoke, it wasn't about him, or his past, or her injuries.

"We almost had it. That creature," Glannon said, punching the tent pole enough to make the whole thing wobble, and he realized with sudden clarity that she was angry. Furious. "And then you let go."

"I tried to hold on," he said.

Now she turned to face him, her brows knit. A line stood out starkly in the shadows, right between her eyes. Her mother had similar wrinkles as he remembered her. A proud woman, too. But Glannon had cracks, cracks that weren't there before what happened to Yuri.

"Do you remember the last time you touched me?" she asked him.

He could tell she was purposely avoiding his name. And there was no use lying to her.

"I'm sorry," he said. "I know that's not enough. But I'm sorry."

"It's not… it's not that you did it, exactly, that stayed with me so long," she said, folding her arms across her chest, wincing as she did so. "It's what you said. When you pinned me against that tree."

"I was foolish. And drunk. Doesn't excuse it."

"Those words. Do you remember them?" She wasn't going to give up. "Because I do."

Goddess, she was going to make him say them again.

He closed his eyes. "I said that when I was mormaer, when my father's disease finally ate him up from the inside, that I could take you whenever I wanted. Make you my whore."

Her eyes filled with tears. Glannon Bel. Crying. Because of something he'd said to her seven years ago. He'd hit her with practice swords harder than he'd hit Caxigo. He'd called her names. He'd played tricks on her and watched from the bushes. Child's play. And she'd never cried. But those words, drunken and mad, were the most brutal. And why had he said it? Because he was jealous of her and wanted to make her afraid.

"And that's why I left you to die, Braig Vann. Lon the Boar, whoever you are now," she said. "Because, yes. I've always been an ambitious brat. I'm my mother's child, and she was a cold, cruel bitch, even if everyone keeps forgetting. Did she not kill our grandfather to take the seat as mormaer before it was outlawed? But when I had the chance, when I could edge you into the Wothwood and let it decide to take you…"

He nodded. He understood.

She took a breath and continued. "I knew you would make a poor ruler. I knew that you would use your power to bring to heel those who dared challenge you, and I knew that I would fight you with every breath I had, even if it meant all out rebellion. Even if it tore the Bright Banner clan apart. But I also knew you would make good on that promise you made me that night. And if not, the threat would have been enough to drive me mad."

Her tears did not reach her voice, damn her. If he'd had been crying, his voice would have been as wobbly as an old crone's.

"The diadem was never mine to have," he said, holding out his hands as if offering to the goddess herself. He tried to fill his words with all sincerity. "As you said, I have no inheritance."

Glannon laughed coldly, shaking her head, tears still trekking down her dirty cheeks. "But don't you see? I *lied* to you."

Lon's head snapped up. "What?"

"I wanted you to die *hurting*. I wanted to take away what made you most proud. Your name. Your inheritance. I wanted to strip you bare and fill you with sorrow as your life blood returned to the earth."

Lon swallowed. He let her words sink in. Let down his hands. Looked at his hands. Looked at her.

She kept talking. "My mother told me, many times over, that every man fears his mother was a harlot, that his father is some wandering soldier or tyckner. Only women can truly know, by tracing their line to Noduuoret, as I have."

"I don't…" started Lon, then stopped, letting it settle in.

"The battle joy," Glannon said, holding out her hands, wiggling her fingers. "You must have forgotten. And, to be honest, I did, too. Until Per Carro explained it. It's an old story, about how the descendants of the goddess can channel her power when they're together. That's what runs in the veins of the children of Noduuoret. That's what we felt, when we touched. It was the gift she gave her children, to give succor to the dying and strength to the weary. When we…"

Now he wanted to kill her. Just a little bit, but it was enough. The flame of hate rekindled.

"… Marchan Vann came from the line of Noduuoret, and he was your father. Your mother was a Kurui, the weaver class. You could have only inherited this gift from him."

She'd *lied* to him.

He had to keep reminding himself to breathe. Because if he was so stupid to have believed the words of an ambitious fourteen-year-old who left him to die, he was stupid enough to forget that he needed air to live.

Then he stood, towering over Glannon.

She stared him down, unafraid.

"Good night, Glannon Bel," he said. "The Wothwood awaits us both the morning."

"But Braig, we need to talk about the gift. The battle joy. If we're to go into the wood together, we have to make it work."

"Fuck the Wothwood. And fuck yourself, mormaer."

"Braig, please…"

But he didn't hear the last words coming from her because he was already out into the cold night air, moving as quickly away from her as he could go. He shouldered past Per Madoc on his way, heard words of challenge behind him, but he simply kept walking until he came into view of the tyckner's caravans.

Braig had hoped that upon seeing the tyckners he'd feel a sense of belonging, but instead he felt like he was seeing them for the first time. In the light of the bonfire, the windows shone like strange eyes, candlelight behind them winking as if in knowing.

Daybreak the next morning, Braig stood among the gathered group, having not slept. Rather than sleep among the tyckners, he'd walked the perimeter of the camp a dozen times over, perhaps hoping to coax whatever had attacked them earlier into showing itself, to get a better look at the enemy. Not for Glannon, but for himself. He wanted to understand it, to prepare for the trip into the Wothwood.

But it didn't show. In a most amusing contrast to the violence of the previous day, the wood was quiet, demure, as if it had spent too much of its anger stitching together that monstrosity to fight them.

Twelve were assembled. Poole and another tyckner named Wystan. Aoda Kanna, Lieutenant Shenbar, and four other soldiers. Most of good rank and experience, judging by the sheer amount of embroidery on their uniforms. They looked tired but not afraid. Then came Caxigo, Per Carro, and Glannon.

He tried not to watch the way that Glannon leaned into Per Madoc as they spoke, the way he took her hand and kissed it. He tried not to think of where he fit in the whole matter nor what it meant to Poole.

Poole, for his part, stood just to the side of the gathered party. He carried very little compared to what Braig was used to seeing him with on trips. Just a large satchel, curiously unadorned, and his best clothes. He wore a long, thick cloak to keep out the chill and topped the whole business with his wide-brimmed hat. If he was nervous or concerned, it did not show.

Damned Poole. Always acting as if he was part of his own personal hero story.

For a moment Braig thought that the man was going to take note of him, give him a look of solidarity. But he did not. He simply looked straight ahead as Captain Moll came into view, high atop his horse, the shoulder plumes of his station making him look broader than he was.

Judging by the stubble on his chin and the stains on his uniform, Braig suspected he might have had too much to drink the night before.

"Citizens and soldiers of Theria," said Captain Moll.

Braig was wrong. He hadn't had too much to drink *before*. He'd already had too much to drink. The man was drunk.

Lieutenant Shenbar blinked, and Braig could tell he was doing his best to contain his embarrassment.

Moll cleared his throat. As if that would help the slurring. "You go forth into a great unknown, but I have prayed nightly for your safety and… gods," he said, reaching up and pressing on the bridge of his nose. He was that drunk. "Just don't get killed because the future of… of all of Theria is in your hands."

There was no further ado. Moll swayed on his horse, and one of his squires reached up to steady him as he went back the short distance they came.

The small crowd that had gathered dissipated as quickly as it had come together.

"I bet you're feeling quite proud to be Therian right now," came Aoda Kanna's voice from Braig's shoulder. "That was the send-off of a generation."

"I could smell the liquor from here," Braig replied. "What's got to him?"

Aoda raised her eyebrows and lowered her voice. "I'm fairly sure he's convinced he's sent us to our death and doom, and the only way they'll get what they want is by plowing the forest to the ground with the whole army. So, he's sending Shenbar to get killed, and they're good friends. But there's no way out of it. He came to try and convince me otherwise, but I don't think we're going to die, even if the captain is too frightened by local tales to think otherwise."

"There is one more thing we need to attend to!" came Poole's voice above the other hushed conversations.

He dug into his bag, rummaging around for something, and then pulled out a handful of buttons. Most of them were made of a silver metal and looked, otherwise, rather unimpressive. Battered, beaten, dented in a hundred places. But as Poole came toward Braig and handed him one, he noticed that they'd been fashioned into pins. Regardless of their state, they were still metal—hard to come by—and fashioned rather beautifully.

"Keep these on, no matter what," said Poole as he helped Aoda fasten hers, right near her heart. "No matter what."

Chapter Eleven
Graves

THEY WERE NOT FAR FROM THE WO RIVER, SO IT ONLY TOOK A HALF DAY'S walk for the small company to arrive at the border of the Wothwood. Braig could hear the rushing waters before he saw them. Familiar sounds. Strange that even though he'd been in a mad dash to kill a boar the last time he'd come through, it felt as if he'd never stopped listening to it. Both a great comfort to him and then, immediately, a sense of revulsion.

He kept quiet as Aoda Kanna and one of the other soldiers did some surveying, measuring the distance between rocks for all he knew, with string and poles and little devices. Glannon was there, still and silent, overseeing the business as if she had some idea of what was going on, Caxigo speaking softly to her every now and again. The mormaer had yet to make eye contact with him since last night's revelation. Was she finally feeling a little bit of guilt? Did it matter?

Turning to watch the surveyors, Braig didn't think Aoda's heart was in it, but once she'd written down some scribbles in her notebook, she indicated that the striations and sediment in this area confirmed her suspicions that they needed to go in a roughly north easterly direction.

Poole knew the way and agreed on the course. Together they walked parallel to the sandy banks, boots scraping with the sediment, until they arrived at a narrower passage across the river. One side was the Briarwood, safety. The other bank was the Wothwood, only nightmares and hearsay.

"This is it," said Poole, and went across without so much as a blink. He called back over his shoulder, halfway through, "Just go straight. Straight through. No deviation."

Wystan, the other tyckner, followed on his heels.

No one else moved, though. No one wanted to follow suit so blindly, so carelessly.

Then Aoda Kanna crossed. Without word, without even a gesture, she simply forded the shallow river bed, stones slick with moss and algae, until she stood upon the opposite shore, looking around.

The rest stared at her, but Braig was just a few steps behind. Perhaps out of a sense of duty or protection, or simply friendship, he did not want her to be alone on that side too long. Not with two tyckners.

As he walked across the river, he felt the cool water seep into his boots, and he remembered fishing with his father. He almost slipped on some of the rocks, just as he had as a boy, getting lost looking at the eddies and rivulets around his boots.

When he reached Aoda, she looked relieved and breathed, "Oh, there you are… for a moment there…"

"She was worried she was stuck with us forever," Poole drawled. "Just a trick of the light, I'm sure."

Aoda pointed across the river, and he understood. The other bank was invisible, hung thick with mist the same color as the grey morning.

He took her hand, so small in his, and nodded down at her. "I'm here," he said. "And they'll come."

Glannon was next, Caxigo and Per Carro right behind her. Then the soldiers and Shenbar. All experienced a similar concern upon crossing the bank. Some reported seeing fog or mist; others swore it was smoke so thick it made them cough uncontrollably, burning their mouths and throats.

Braig looked around to get a better feel for the place. As of that moment, he did not feel different. There was no more dread in him than before, no more fear. No sense of less control, or communication with the divine.

Maybe it was a little colder here, a little darker. But woods were woods.

The trees were, more or less, the same as they had been on the other side, but there was a significantly less sense that anyone—or anything—had been by in recent years. If ever. The wood had a deep smell to it, loamy and mineral, and a wetness to it. Braig still shivered in the morning air, but if he hadn't only walked a few paces, he'd have thought it had either just rained or was about to rain.

It didn't feel familiar, Braig didn't think. Not in the way he had expected.

Without a word, they began walking, Poole at the head. Whatever truth there was to find, it was out there, with Noduuoret's Grave.

Thirty-six.
Thirty-seven.

Thirty-eight… no, still seven. The leaves on those last two were the same. Just a trick of the light.

Aoda tried to keep track of all the flora she had not marked before, mostly to keep her mind off the fact that she had, arguably, led these eleven souls to their doom. It worked for a time, this categorization and observation, but it was quickly getting out of hand. The first discovery happened not long after they crossed the Wo River, a downy clover that she was certain was heretofore undiscovered. Not that botany was her primary research by any means, but she had gone through advanced classes before she had arrived in Brezhia. No self-respecting surveyor would ignore what the plants could tell.

It was a good distraction, even if it only gave her more empirical evidence that everything was wrong with the Wothwood. The season didn't even feel right. Sure, it was cold. But the chill did not appear to concern the trees, none of which had shed their leaves. They looked like trees she knew, and yet they did not behave as they should. Everything lived in a state of slowness; there was almost no sign of decay about them, but neither was their growth.

"Keep the line," Poole said, a few paces ahead of Aoda. He was insistent that they keep in a line, much to the consternation of the soldiers. He said it was safer and that was how he and his people had made the journey before.

"What is that?" asked Aoda, pointing ahead.

From a distance, she had thought it was some kind of rock, dark and looming. At least that was what she kept telling herself. A rock was a very safe thing to imagine. Stable and, at that size, immovable. Some strange geological anomaly. Except, as she continued closer to it, she could not account for the size. At this distance, it would have to be higher than any building in Yereva.

Lon—Braig, she reminded herself. He'd asked her to start using that name if she could. And it did fit him better.

"Wait." Braig might not have been commanding the company, but they still listened to him. His voice had a way of being soft and yet impossible to miss at the same time.

Aoda felt the hair on the back of her neck go up.

"Don't break the line," Poole warned. "That's the way we do things in the Wothwood. Lots of distractions. If you feel strange, off, just touch your button."

"I know where we are," said Braig.

A glance back at the mormaer and Aoda could assume that went for her, too.

"But this wasn't…" said Glannon Bel, looking confused. "We weren't that far from the river. You said you were on the bank of the river." She added that last bit rather quickly, her steely visage slipping just for a second.

Aoda knew well what she meant. She'd left him on the bank of the river.

Poole sighed as if schooling a group of children. "Of course not. That was a long time ago. Things here move. They slip. Rivers aren't allowed to move like you and I? Pish. We've got one thing to focus on now, and we need to do it collectively. If you start daydreaming, we'll all end up dead."

"The buzzing hurts my brain," said one of the soldiers.

"It's worse than you know. You're protected now from the bulk of it—these resonators do the trick." He poked at the button on his lapel, the one silver among a sea of other colors. Aoda touched hers in response, contemplating what he meant exactly. She did feel a little better when her skin touched the metal.

"Resonators?" she asked him.

"Yes, that's what we call them, at least. Our technology might not move mountains, but it's grown out of necessity. Tiny workings due to our tiny resources. It's been ages of work getting these to do their job and consistently. So long as we stay in the line, we're… well, shit cakes, I said stay in the line!"

"Something up ahead, sir," said someone behind her.

The expletive was directed at one of the soldiers who had left the line to get a closer look at something off the beaten path, a wide rock or fallen log. As of yet he had not turned to a pillar of stone or attracted any unwarranted attention, but Aoda couldn't help but feel nervous.

The soldier frowned into the continual dusk, pointing his spear, but taking a step back to fall into place. "That's a boar, or I'm not Yerevan," he said. "But it's not moving."

"It's not just any boar," said Braig. "That's the one that should have killed me."

"But it's been seven years," said Glannon Bel.

Aoda squinted against the cognitive dissonance in her mind. It actually hurt. The pressure behind her eyes, the pain in her temples.

"What's your theory, Professor?" Poole asked, goading her.

"There are two possibilities. One, it is a boar. Any boar. That recently died. Braig could be mixed up about where he last was. That wouldn't be the first time someone's lost their bearings due to an emotional experience," she said. "Secondly, well, this is a wild guess, but there are some gasses and compounds known to slow growth, or more accurately, preserve flesh. The soil samples will take a long time for me to examine, but it's possible that the boar ingested too much of said components and, upon death, mummified."

"Either way, I wouldn't go exploring," Shenbar warned the soldier.

"You have answers for everything, Aoda Kanna," Poole said with a smirk. "Though it might serve you well some places, it won't here. Why couldn't it be the same boar?"

"Because it would have died seven years ago," she said.

"And yet, this whole place feels as if it's holding its breath, doesn't it?" Poole asked. "Even you can't deny that."

Aoda didn't want to lie. Lying felt wrong here. Everything felt wrong here. She felt wrong here. She bit down on her lip until she felt a trickle of blood.

"There's got to be a logical explanation," Aoda said at last, wishing that Poole would just stop talking to her.

As they passed by the dead boar, Aoda shivered. It might as well have been carved of stone, but indeed showed no sign of decomposition anywhere. The moss and grass about it looked recently stirred, as if someone—two or three someones—had been standing around it. One pair of tracks led away.

She looked over at Glannon Bel again.

"Look, there are red flowers," said Poole, pointing to the little blossoms springing out from beneath the boar. They looked like violets but were the color of blood. Blossoming blood. "You should come up with a name for them, Professor."

Blood violets, she thought without a moment's pause.

They continued their march along the banks of the Wo River and deeper into the Wothwood, still single file, each waiting for some glimpse or indication of the change of day. They had turned abruptly to the north when the river did the same, and the sight of the strange shape in the distance vanished. But no sun rose, nor did it set. It remained cold and sunless, but the thick vegetation did not seem to notice.

And how strange it was, Aoda thought, that there was little to no obstruction. No fallen logs, treacherous paths. Poole sang softly to himself from time to time, Wystan joining in with him when the mood set. But no one knew the tyckner songs, and so they went mostly unaccompanied.

Then Aoda noticed movement, precisely the same time that most of the others did. And light, too. Away to her left, there was a clearing. Shapes swirled in and out of view, and she could see the suggestion of buildings. High spires and sprawling palisades.

"No, don't go that way," Poole said, turning around and facing the gathered group. "Just pretend it isn't there."

"Poole?" asked Aoda. "What is it?"

He did not miss a beat, but said softly, "It's nothing I can explain to you with words or reason. So ignore it. Look away. You are the only one that sees that reality, and I implore everyone—" he raised his voice at this so everyone could hear, "—to press hard upon the resonators and follow the feet in front of you. Do not ask questions, do not describe what you see. Just continue walking."

"But I can't. I..." Aoda stammered, her throat tightening, stomach churning. The ground no longer felt safe. It felt soft, yielding, like flesh. She would fall.

Think. Think. Logic. You must have... eaten some bad food. Mushrooms, perhaps, someone put in your food. Poole poisoned you and...

Her eyes wouldn't follow her logic. She was drawn to the clearing, which, from what she could see, now surrounded them on both sides. It was as if the wood had shrunk and thinned, flanked by the impossible. On one side there still remained the castles, but now she could see immense creatures flying in and out of the parapets. Dragons. It was hard to know for certain between all the thick foliage, and even so, it had a blurred quality to it, as if someone had smeared a glass with lard.

Aoda's legs began to feel strange. Heavy. The feeling was akin to the times she'd lost circulation in her legs, that strange pins and needles sensation. And yet she took notice that the sensation spread up every time she looked to her left or to her right.

The ruins to her right were just a void. No, not entirely. It was a great, black, impossible night filled with stars so cold she wished for death.

Poole's voice came to her out of her mounting panic, a voice piercing and far away. Even though he was right before her.

"Tell me about your theory," he said. "About Noduuoret's Grave. You said you spent all night putting it together."

That darkness. That void. That never thinking nothing nothing…

"Aoda Kanna."

Poole's voice startled her.

"Your theory. Tell us all. As loud as you can."

They murmured behind her. Caxigo was weeping. Shenbar mentioned something about giant turkeys.

There is always an explanation.

The button at her lapel pulsed as she touched it, welcoming her back to whatever approximation of reality she'd found herself in.

"Yes," she said at last, her voice muffled in her own ears. "I do have a theory."

That was right. She had a theory. Grounded in science, though it felt painfully limited.

Behind her, she heard someone stumble, and Poole added, "Loud enough for everyone to hear!"

"A meteor," Aoda said, recalling the sheaves of paper she'd drawn her equations on. Words were difficult to follow, but if she dug down enough, she could remember. "Perhaps… made of some kind of element, yes, that would attract metal to it in large quantities. A single impact, burrowing deep underground. Some kind of magnetism that works on most metals, especially iron and copper, since those were the most depleted… If Noduuoret was indeed magical, there could have been some collision. Especially if her sword was made of that rarest of metals…"

Listening to Aoda helped. Glannon didn't quite know what to think of the half-breed Brezhian woman with that horribly malformed face, but she did like her voice. It was difficult to understand most of what she was talking about—now she was discussing the magnetic properties of iron, nickel, and cobalt—but following that line of science helped to pull Glannon's mind from where they were exactly.

Because it was too much for her to see. The words helped the horrors around them fade.

Even if she didn't see those glimpsed vistas, there was enough in this part of the Wothwood to concern her. For one, there were bite marks on a tree she passed. Shark bites. She knew the pattern well enough from raids to the shore. How unfathomable.

And the view. Every turn of their path, painfully in file, brought them to a new view just out of view of the trees. How improbable it all seemed, and yet strangely familiar. As if she'd dreamed it a hundred times and was just now remembering.

Braig was in front of her, Per Carro behind. The per was breathing heavily, just a hint of a wheeze on the inhale.

But they kept walking.

Even when two of Shenbar's soldiers vanished, followed by the sound of crunching.

Even when Aoda's voice went away, and came back, and sounded like starlight.

Even when the pathway turned to water. Then to sand. Then back again.

"Keep moving forward," Poole kept saying, his voice as smooth and true as river stones, cool and collected. "Resonate. *Resonate.*"

Then they were all singing a song. A Brezhian song. Perhaps Braig started it, she couldn't recall. But the words helped.

Oh star, oh star, Noduuoret fair
Upon the broken, battered land
A sword sundered, a promise given
Oh star, oh star, Noduuoret fair
Mother of a thousand clans and
Sister of the forest stream
Oh star, oh star, Noduuoret fair

Glannon had not felt the need to draw her weapon until the song finished, though she could not owe it to anything she saw, exactly. Now it was firm in her hand, the grip warming to her touch. Because something was wrong.

They had just passed through a sandy stretch of land, spindly trees sticking out at every angle and burned, tufted grass grasping at their waists. The going was difficult as the sand was soft and deep in places. Dust billowed and got into her eyes, crusted in her hair. If the company hadn't been coughing before, they were coughing now.

Poole showed no sign of flagging until they crossed to a rockier section of land, the trees thicker and more familiar to her. And yet the air chilled, shivered perceptibly. It was like heat waves from a distance, yet cold as snow.

Glannon felt a presence. A palpable pressure. She thought of Per Madoc, of his mad, beautiful eyes, praying to the goddess that she hadn't been followed. Praying that he had heeded her words, in spite of his efforts to the contrary. Oh, he'd made such a fury when she had forbidden him and taken Per Carro instead. What would he think of her praying? What would he make of this place?

"Poole," Glannon said, shoving his shoulder. "What is this?"

The tyckner sniffed the air, said something low to Wystan, his comrade, too low to hear, or else in an unfamiliar language.

"Draw your weapons," Poole said. He said it without inflection, just a simple statement.

Before she could act, something ran into Glannon, invisible to her eyes. The impact was so sudden and powerful that she collided into Braig, his elbow cracking into her helm. Her head ached immediately, teeth grinding against each other, but her years of training kicked in and she steadied herself, planting her feet in a defensive stance and holding her blades up.

Wystan gurgled something incomprehensible, then reached into his satchel. Shenbar growled into the dim wood, ready to fight, but clearly unsure how to proceed. How could they fight an invisible force?

Again, it came at Glannon, this time barreling into her back, sharp and pointed between her shoulder blades. She blinked through the sweat in her eyes, looking for her assailant, but seeing only Braig's lumbering form before her, his expression as confused as she felt.

Then came a spray of dust, tinged with a red hue and sparkling as it settled. The other tyckner, Wystan, was responsible. He'd always carried a variety of pouches, but it was difficult to decipher from his general eccentricity of dress. Now, Glannon had an idea why.

As the dust settled, it revealed shapes, revealing their forms in a single, rusty hue. The one responsible for hitting Glannon was vaguely man-like, though instead of feet, it had the bare suggestion of tendrils. Which wouldn't have been so off-putting were it not easily twice her height. Perhaps it had two heads. Perhaps it had teeth and claws. Wystan's magic trick did not allow for such detail, and that sense of insubstantial matter made Glannon's skin crawl.

Even after fighting Yuri, she preferred to fight creatures she could see and understand. Not moving, writing masses.

Fear would have to wait because survival kicked in. Never the warrior to turn tail and leave, she anchored her stance and moved forward, swinging her swords to make contact with the relative center of the creature, somewhere about her shoulders.

Her swords passed through with no resistance, and the mass of chalky red dust compressed and then blew out again, now taking on another form.

"Hit the red part," shouted Wystan, as if Glannon's attempt was as effective as yanking at the prick of a ram for milk.

The red part? It was all red, what she could see. And now the creatures were swirling about them. Shenbar made a heroic attempt to crush a tentacle beneath his boot, but it simply slid away, converging again into a new monstrous shape, now with two heads, mouths wide open.

They were angry.

But they were familiar.

Glannon went to block a blow from above, catching not the shadow but Braig's warning, and took in a big breath of air. Except with the inhalation came that dust and…

Every step and memory together we cry and stay and die and rot upon the earth here… All together a thousand voices waiting until the living give us life again… The eyes and the tongues of the still host, the great host, the blind host, fumbling in darkness where steel and shard is nothing… but whispers and memory together we cry and stay and die and rot upon the earth here…

She dropped her swords because she understood. *Where steel and shard is nothing.*

As the hulking creature reamassed before her, Glannon hopped to her left then her right, remembering sparring with Braig before she was big enough to manage a glass weapon. It wasn't easy to fell him, but there was always a weak point.

Wystan continued to weave in and out, throwing red dust to cover the creatures.

"Use your fists!" Glannon shouted above the din, her throat dry and raspy from the dust. Her head felt heavy, her eyelids drowsy. The echoing voices still lingered. Yelling helped.

Then she punched at the creature, somewhere behind one of its knees. This time, the blow made contact. Her enemy shuddered and collapsed to one side, and she kept raining punches upon it, now beset with a frenzy beyond her reckoning. It might have been the tyckner's dust, or else some long dormant capability, but whatever the cause, she could not stop once she began her flurry of attacks. Each time her fist connected, she was rewarded with a sickening crunch, like brittle leaves over cracked leather. Sometimes there came a spray of blood. And it was satisfying to her very core, as quenching as cold water after a hunt, as perfect as a climax after rutting. She began to lose herself in it.

Glannon gasped as one of the partially-visible creatures came at her from behind, wrapping around her waist to pull her back. But she bit at it, furious and snarling, her mouth filling with a sticky, bitter substance. Then she was free and fighting again until…

"Glannon. Mormaer!"

She came out of the red mists, blinking as if rising from a long dream. Around her lay desiccated animal bodies, holes right through them. Hairless, to a number, but recognizable: bears, horses, foxes, and more besides. Their corpses bloated and veined.

Per Carro was at her side, staring into her eyes. "You killed them all."

"They were already dead," Poole intoned.

"How… how?" asked Aoda, in the distance, sounding as if she were talking to someone else. "The animation was… the way they fell apart and then…"

Glannon wiped her face, looked at her gauntlets. They were black to her elbows with sticky fluids.

"Someone fell out of line," said Poole. "Best not do it again. The dead remember, and they come for us when we stray. It's a good thing the mormaer here had the right idea."

"You killed them all," Braig said softly, looking upon the refuse with the same bemused expression he'd had the night he'd seen her. "You were impressive."

Per Carro's hands trembled as he held out her weapons. Glannon grabbed them and shoved past them, tightening her armor and nodding to Poole. "If everyone is alive, let us move on."

"What were those things?" Aoda Kanna asked, looking to Glannon for hope. "How did you do such a thing?"

"It doesn't matter. They're dead now."

"But, mormaer, surely we should take some samples and tend to you. You don't know what's in the fluid—"

"No. We're done here. I swallowed it, and I'm not dead yet, so let's move. And if anyone else falls out of line, I'll personally see to it that they join our hairless friends here."

How long they walked, she did not know. Time and thought and dream melded together. The fight left her ill at ease, but more deeply attuned to her senses than ever before. The landscape didn't matter as it had before, did not bother her. Though she did not speak of it to her companions, she had a growing sense that it was but the death pangs of an already festering body, now riddled with wounds. At the heart lay her inheritance, the inheritance of her people: Noduuoret's Grave and, perhaps, a great city beyond. That mattered more than all else. More than the safety of her people, more than her life.

At some point, she reached out and Braig's hand was already there, meeting her halfway, interrupting her dark thoughts with a welcome squeeze. Glannon didn't understand how he would want to touch her, or how he had ended up nearby, but the connection was instant and welcome. Her vision flushed with new clarity, her resolve deepened. Together, they had more power. She could not forget that.

"Poole says we're almost there," Braig said to her. He didn't need to speak the words, but he did anyway.

"You're afraid," she told him, because it was true.

"You're changing. This place… it's part of you, isn't it? What you did there before. With those invisible creatures. Glannon, you have to know it was the most incredible fight I've ever seen. I didn't even have time to react."

"I did what I had to do," she said. Perhaps she ought to have felt proud, but the praise felt meaningless. "To get us to what is ours. To find out why Noduuoret left us."

"What if it's nothing? What if this is a trap?" asked Braig. "I know they have other reasons to be here. You know that, too."

They were now speaking without words, out of fear that the tyckners would overhear them.

"Yes, I know. But the gift they give me will be greater."

She knew she didn't say "us" but that was because it would have been a lie. "My mother's blood is here," she said to Braig. "I'm closer to her than I have been since she left. It makes me strong where they are weak."

Ahead, tall trees swayed in the breeze, and the company came to a stop. There was a good deal of discussion between Wystan and Poole before the latter turned to the company.

"We have arrived," Poole said. "At long last, and through a bit of a challenge, we have but a few steps to take before entering the ground of Noduuoret's Grave."

For the first time, Glannon heard something curious in his voice. Hesitation. Excitement. Fear. There was nothing in front of them, but then there was. No steps were taken, no physical travel, but the wood itself opened up, parting like a curtain, to show what remained hidden.

Noduuoret's Grave. And the great city she guarded.

A mist roiled about their feet, colder than the air. Then it rose, tickling Glannon's nose and moving her hair.

She was standing next to Braig, now, breaking the line as they all had without command. Poole was positioned in the middle of their cluster, a little bit ahead, Wystan just beside him.

Poole took a deep breath and then turned to them, his long-fingered hands splayed wide as if in offering to some great, unseen god.

Glannon didn't like the look on Poole's face. She didn't know the man well, but years of sitting on the Chair of Rule had taught her to learn the lines of a person's face as swiftly as possible. In Bannercliffe, any judgement she made had consequences. She had to live near, and sometimes even do business with, the accused. Their bodies would often tell different stories than their words.

Except this time, she had the suspicion that Poole would tell the story now. Their journey was, in some ways, too easy. They had been prepared for another Yuri incident, or at least a living boar or two to contend with.

"Well," said Poole, looking from face to face when no one moved. "I have brought you to Noduuoret's Grave. Just past this copse of trees, affectionately known at the Goddess's Loins, is her final resting place."

"What are we doing, then?" Shenbar asked. "You just expect us to traipse in there? We've hardly had food or sleep or a moment to speak to each other. It's preposterous. We need a plan."

Glannon felt irritated by the man, yet glad she could feel that emotion. The memory of what she had endured on her way to this place was fading, and she felt her own self return. Like an embryo back to its shell. But there was an enduring hardness still, one that the fight with the dead creatures had given her that she began to think of as perfect. She had always liked fighting, but she had craved it there, sated herself on it. Glannon had become monstrous, and it did not frighten her as much as it made her curious.

"Lieutenant, are you truly that keen on storming the place when we've just endured so much?" Glannon gestured vaguely behind them. "Need I describe what we've been through?"

"What matters is that we *lived through* it," Shenbar said, glancing at his own men, now diminished to two. "Most of us, anyway."

"I *said* stay in a line," Poole reiterated. "I don't think they quite grasped the severity of the situation. Traversing the *frey* will do that to a person, though. And I regret not giving you the details, it's only that everyone interprets it differently, and once everyone starts talking at once, panic sets in. The buttons, of course, protect you to a certain extent, but trying to describe ahead of time would have been a waste."

Aoda Kanna looked particularly small, shrinking into her hood. Trembling. Whatever she had seen clearly had shaken her. Glannon wanted to hold her hand, too, but she was too far off.

"What's the frey?" asked Glannon, once Poole's words settled in.

"I didn't tell you?" asked Poole. "I could have sworn I did."

"No, you didn't tell us anything about a frey," she replied.

Poole tilted his head at her, as if seeing her for the first time. Then he composed himself. "Yes, right. It must have been your mother I was thinking of."

Now it was Glannon's turn to breathe heavily. Per Carro stiffened behind her. Braig squeezed her hand tightly. They were both afraid of her, afraid of what she might do. But they weren't wrong. She was not against the idea of punching Poole to a pulp.

"My mother's been dead for over twenty years," Glannon said. She struggled to keep her voice even, but it was quite a task. She was so tired.

Poole counted on his fingers. "I suppose that would be right. Hard to keep track, honestly. But I didn't mention that I knew her?"

"You left that part out, rather conveniently." Braig spoke the words. He didn't know either, and that made her feel better.

"Well, I was able to convince her to come into the frey as well. It's not the Wothwood; it's part of the Wothwood. I thought, being descended from Noduuoret, that she might be the key to fixing the *problem*, but there was more that needed to be done. She didn't have the right breeding," explained Poole. "Or perhaps it was temperament. Regardless, it's what got her in the end."

He said all of this so matter-of-factly that Glannon found it difficult to understand.

"*You* killed my mother?" Anger flared in her, and it felt good. Felt right. It was as if the whole of the Wothwood flared with her.

And maybe it did.

The ground pulsed red, Braig's hand hot in hers. She would burn it all down.

Poole nodded his head as if in approval. "I'm sorry," he said. "But this is all bigger than you. Thankfully, as we proved before, you and he are the right breeding and the right temperament. Blood magic is rudimentary at best, but it is hard to get around."

Shenbar pressed forward, Aoda on his heels. "This is an affront to the whole of the Empire," he said. "You'll be hanged for treason as soon as you're returned."

Oh, Ori Shenbar.

The wood itself seemed to say it.

Poole shrugged. "I'm but a man trying to solve a problem. A mutual problem. You want ore and riches. I want to fix this gate, this door between worlds. It doesn't concern you directly, so I didn't think the details necessary. I can deliver for you if you deliver for me. And to do this, I had to know you could take care of the… *challenges* closing the portal would pose. Challenges I can't possibly manage on my own. The fact that you're all still alive is remarkable!"

Braig leaned forward faster than Glannon could react, punching Poole in the face. It was not a direct command, and yet... Teeth flew out with a spray of blood, but Poole bounded back up as if nothing had happened, wiping at his mouth.

"This is a sacred place," Glannon said, fury still upon every syllable. The ground was warm beneath her feet, a commanding power rising up inside of her.

"I *agree*!" Poole said, his voice nearing a shriek. "But becoming holy ground is what caused all this trouble, which I'm trying to fix—and, mind you, keep as many prying eyes from the situation as possible. If you kill me, which I can see is quickly becoming an option, you won't be able to fix the gate. The gate will be forever belching nonsense out into the Wothwood. The Brezhians will forever be stuck as insular savages with little glass weapons and big egos, and Yereva will never stop breathing down their necks."

"You need to explain this better, Poole," said Braig. "Or I will spill your guts for you."

"Not if I get there first," growled Shenbar.

"Start at the beginning," Braig said to Poole. And for a brief moment, and for the first time he could recall, Poole looked frightened of him.

The tyckner looked at Wystan, who still had yet to utter a word during the trip, other than his strange singing. They exchanged a glance, nodded at each other.

"The lore of Brezhia says that some two thousand years ago, a goddess named Noduuoret came into the Wothwood to save her people. Now, I don't know precisely what happened in that moment, but from that time on, coming into the wood was forbidden," Poole explained. "Do I have that bit right?"

Braig nodded. "More or less."

Glannon was breathing softly by his side, her hand still in his. Wet and warm. She did not want to let go, and he did not want her to. He felt anchored when she was there.

"Good. Now, something occurred—and you will see it soon enough—in that act. Whether it was science or the true divine, I'm not certain," Poole explained, glancing at Aoda. "The professor here has a curious theory, which I could certainly rule as plausible. If a goddess was struck by a meteor, or some other heavenly body—or simply expelled enough force to... well, disrupt the very fabric of time and place—that would explain what we're seeing. The magnetism caused a tremendous kind of reverse shockwave, bringing ore toward this very place during impact. Aoda knows the stories of mines crumpling into the earth and weapons traveling miles before being found again."

He took a deep breath, and then Braig heard something behind him, coming from the direction of the copse of trees. It was the sound of breathing and sucking at the same time. Fleshy, like giant lungs straining for breath.

"Tyckners aren't just common here in the Empire, or Luthland. We exist…" He trailed off, wincing as the sucking sound continued, wheezing. The trees moved with it. "Across many planes. We are the keepers of great technology and secrets. And we have been studying this gate because it is broken. Quite broken."

"We've been studying this area for years. Generations. And we believe that the Wothwood has been split, broken—twisted into frey," Wystan added.

"You keep saying that word," Aoda said, bristling. "You've yet to define it for us."

"Do you know what a labyrinth is?" asked Poole.

Aoda hissed in annoyed response. Braig knew the one point of pride on that woman was when someone assumed she didn't know something she did.

"Of course she knows what a fucking labyrinth is," said Braig.

Poole leveled him with an even stare. "Good, well, the frey is the walls of the labyrinth. The space in between. It wasn't always the Wothwood, and the Wothwood may not be the only world within the walls. But we walked as we did because if we were to err, we would have seen more than you are capable of understanding. A billion corners of the labyrinth. Infinite gates," Poole explained. "You already saw enough, I'll warrant. Though it's always hard to remember once you get to this point…"

"We want to fix this gate," said Wystan. "And return home. We can never make it a predictable gate again, for that is a rarity across all the planes, but if we can remove the obstructions, we can at least reverse the…"

His words were swallowed up by the horrible sounds in the distance. Everyone instinctively huddled closer.

"So you needed soldiers," said Braig, finally putting the pieces together. "And descendants of Noduuoret. And better two than one. But we had to be tested."

"Yuri," growled Glannon.

Wystan winced. "It was necessary. If you could fight something made of this place, you could very well help us to the center, to get to the gate, and to get to your own treasure."

"You called that—creature—to us?" she pressed. "On purpose."

"Yes, but you figured it out. I see you've figured out how best to approach your beloved matriarch," Poole said, gesturing to their still clasped hands. "The battle joy. I had thought it a myth; your mother believed it was a myth."

"Don't you dare say her name," warned Glannon.

Poole shrugged, pointing behind him. "She's still there. Parts of her, anyway."

For all that is holy, Glannon, do not take that bait.

Glannon startled, glaring at Braig.

She had heard him, then. It wasn't just the other way around.

Braig breathed, even and clear. "So even if this works, even if we manage to fend off whatever it is you claim we'll see, how are you going to fix this… gate?"

"Not that it concerns you, Braig," Poole said with a sniff. "But I have the answer right here."

Poole reached into the large satchel at his side. He then pulled out the most complex collection of metal that any of them had ever seen. It must have cost a fortune, and a lifetime to collect. What its purpose was, he had no idea. But it was the size of a small shield and had thousands of buttons upon it. Moving at different intervals. Clocks.

"*Time*," Poole said. "Time will kill it."

Chapter Twelve
Fix

They stood and watched Sid Poole. It was all that could be done in such a situation, the only fathomable course. Aoda recognized the dissonant sensation akin to the time she was poisoned. The event had happened when she was a child, due to her mother's falling out with a particularly high-standing client. The fruits had been meant for her mother, but Aoda was a curious and a sometimes greedy child if she thought no one was looking. Those rosy berries were too much for her to avoid. When the poison hit, it was a combination of euphoria and panic, and she remembered laughing and then crying, and then praying for death. It was a great deal of emotion for a small child of four to endure.

Too much information at once. Aoda could feel her grasp on reality twisting out of reach. How was it that she could find all the right words, but not with Sid Poole? A tyckner.

"That just… looks like a hodgepodge of bits and bobs," she said, gesturing to his device.

"And that's what it is. Except, each bit and bob is attuned to the time of a specific plane. It will act as a disruptor and, hopefully, neutralize the situation here so the gate will no longer be a frothing madness… We just have to get through… well… I suppose you'll see soon enough."

He said something more, but it was swallowed up with more of that fleshy noise coming from behind him.

Then Aoda felt his hand on her arm. Felt the button at her lapel sear with heat. Then the world flew out from under her feet, and Poole said he was sorry, but she was sure he was laughing.

Poole and the professor were gone in a flash of light. Glannon only blinked, and a moment later, they reappeared, deeper into the wood, Wystan next to them, their capes like smoke behind them, slowly materializing

"Stop him!" cried Shenbar, as if that would help.

"What in hells?" asked Braig, which was closer to the right sentiment.

Glannon didn't bother to say anything. It was no longer time for contemplating, for explaining. It was time for action. This was what she was born for.

So she simply looked at Braig, still holding his hand, and then at Caxigo, who nodded in reply; the three took off at a run behind Poole and Aoda. The rest had other agendas, but the Brezhians' was anchored into the land. Theirs was bled into the ground itself.

Her heart pumping, hair streaming behind her, running headlong into the unknown, Glannon Bel felt renewed, reborn. Almost elated. Though the terrain grew spongier as she approached the edge of the wood and her lungs wheezed in protest, blood flow to her body helped her root herself to the few facts that made sense. Aoda Kanna was in trouble. Sid Poole had killed her mother. Sid Poole had killed Yuri.

Sid Poole had orchestrated all of this. If what he said was true, he wasn't even of this world. He was… Glannon didn't have a word for it, but the thought made her uneasy and curious at the same time.

They had just reached the edge of the tree line when she tried to move her hand from Braig's.

But couldn't.

Now a wave of fear washed over her, making her shiver, all her strength and vitality quelling in the face of it. A quick glance down was no help.

She was going to be sick.

Their flesh had mingled, Braig's fingers melting into her own as if fire had sealed them together.

Had she done this? Or had this place done it?

No time.

"There's no time," Braig said to her, his words and her thoughts echoing.

Caxigo put her hand on Glannon's shoulder. "We move, no matter what."

"This is all so damned broken," Glannon said, her voice so loud in her head. Why was she screaming?

"Maybe we're here to fix it," Braig offered. "Maybe we have a chance to fix it for once and all."

She glanced down again in horror at their hands, but he began moving forward. She had no choice other than to follow, a single kando blade at the ready.

Now was the time to be truly brave.

Together, the three Brezhians walked through the thick trees and low-growing vegetation into the space known as Noduuoret's Grave.

Whatever was happening to them, whatever was happening to this place, Braig sensed that Glannon Bel was at the center of it. He knew that without even seeing Noduuoret's Grave itself.

And as they crashed through the brush, he understood why.

Sid Poole hadn't lied.

Braig just hadn't expected to see such a horror.

A gate. A portal. An opening in the earth itself. A crater. All these things.

But made of flesh. And worse. So terrifying that though there were towers in the distance, harbingers of that great lost city, it was no matter. The air churned with wrongness, with stinking brokenness, and all he could do was stare into the crater.

The crater itself looked like an immense metal bowl, the melted ore surrounding the horrific center like a ring. The pale mass within quivered in a vast circle wide enough for ten men to pass through, lined with blood vessels and nerves. But the longer he looked, the more Braig realized: what might have started off as—was this the goddess herself?—was now an amalgam of dozens if not hundreds of creatures. Now fused like the flesh between Glannon and his hands, a multitude of legs, arms, heads, and unidentifiable parts moved, twisted, reached, and blinked. As one they breathed, a tremendous organism knit together with heinous magic taking in the air it needed to live.

It did not end there.

There were people, or rather, parts of people, moving and growing out of this great mass. That's what Poole had meant about Glannon's mother. Some looked as if they were attempting to escape, others looked as if they were trying to crawl back into the mass itself. A strange death and birth, the shriveled flesh pulsing and moving around, undulating like a great tongue. But all connected, just as his hands were to Glannon's.

In the very middle, Braig noticed a blue pulsing center, the light unnaturally bright in the dim of the Wothwood.

"I see my mother's face," Glannon whispered, tears streaking down her face. "Goddess, save us. I am so sorry."

Because she understood, as he did. It was time to fight or be devoured. The goddess gone mad, the world gone mad, and the Wothwood turning in on itself like a great mouth and a great womb at once.

Aoda could barely keep her legs under her as Wystan and Poole ushered her forward toward the horror that was before her. They had awoken whatever lived at the center of the crater. When her feet didn't hit mucus-streaked flesh, they struck upon hard ground. She stole a glance to see metal beneath her feet. Gold beneath the creature that had claimed the Wothwood. And silver, copper, nickel, and a great deal of iron gone red with oxidation, striated in long channels leading to the center.

"Let me go," she managed, her voice barely audible. It was more of a strangled cry than any true plea for help. She was no match for Poole's grip.

"I never accounted for you, Aoda Kanna, but we could use you," said Poole, turning her about, staring at her in the eyes. The wind had whipped his hat off his head and his wispy curls flew about his face. "And you need us."

"If we can neutralize the gate," Wystan said, "the timing is right. The moons are both waxing. A new world awaits."

"A world where your mind is treasured above all," added Poole.

"Let... let me go!" she shouted again.

The madness in Poole's eyes, now kindled, did not abate. "Aoda Kanna, listen to me. You are standing at the precipice of your life. All the questions you've wanted answers to, all the compounds you've wanted to study. I can give them to you! And more. Across endless planes. Civilizations of such heightened technology and learning that you would live a lifetime and understand only a fraction of what they are."

"But the city here..." she managed, seeing the grand gates beyond, knowing there would be treasure there, too, a kind more easily understood.

Poole added, "Libraries that could not fit within the boundaries of the great city of Yereva itself. You will find many things here, but you will not find that."

This made her stop.

"I have a duty," Aoda said, and she was weeping though she didn't know why. "I am under oath to the Lord Re."

"The Lord Re is but a mite on the ass of a great dragon in comparison to what I can show you," Poole said, squeezing her hand. The ground undulated again; balance was getting more difficult. "And when you come with me, you will not be beholden to anyone but yourself. I am giving you a chance to know, to perceive, to experience, beyond the realms of this world."

"I want logic. I want to understand," she babbled.

"And what will you do if you remain here? You will never know. Do you think you could live with that?"

"Goddess… no," she whispered, knowing it to be true.

The tyckner leaned forward so she could hear amidst the din. The braying and the shrieking and the barking and moaning. "But you'll have to trust me. When the gate opens, it will only remain so for a very short time, and then there is no guarantee when it will open again."

Aoda shook her head, more out of a desire to clear her wits than to argue with him. But Poole wasn't paying attention. Shenbar was coming after him, attempting to rescue her, murder in his eyes.

Glannon felt the attack before it happened, pulling Braig down with her, their hands blazing white hot.

They had not yet progressed into the crater itself, but the wood around them was teeming with life and poised for attack. What assembled itself behind Braig was a horror made of bones, its bulk made up of hundreds of vertebrae stacked atop one another like tiny barrels in a brew house, blue lights within the bones blinking and rotating side to side. Its five arms and legs were spinal cords, the interiors still leaking fluid, lashing out at them. It had come from the crater itself, coming together as if by an invisible hand.

Like a giant bone spider, it attacked.

Glannon shouted, turning. She used the kando blade to dismember one of its spinal cord legs, but that did little to slow its attack.

Braig, meanwhile, had shouldered his shield and was doing the best he could to keep the attacks at bay. As the spinal cord arms came down on the heavy cured wood, they splintered. But no sooner did they break than more spun into place.

"There must be something more to this," said Glannon, gritting her teeth as more bone creatures formed out of the flesh and trees about them. Three more. One smaller, made of finger bones and ribcages, whirling like a mace. The others vaguely resembled bears. If bears were made of skulls and kept together by maggots.

She felt a wave of nausea but bit down on it, breathing through her nose. It didn't smell like carrion. It smelled like life. Like the very cradle of life. It was just life gone mad. A goddess gone mad.

Her hand burned where she still clasped Braig, impossibly connected with no escape. Looking at the roiling mass of flesh before her left no doubt in her mind what kind of magic was keeping them knit together.

Noduuoret, Noduuoret. What did you do?

Braig was going to be sick. He couldn't understand what was going on around him. Black spots at the edge of his vision threatened to cover his sight. All he wanted to do was be strong for Glannon, to fight for her because it was the right thing to do and it might prove to her after all… after… fuck, but he couldn't remember.

Then he felt Glannon's presence again, her essence, moving up his arm, through their clasped hands. Her blood, his blood. Somehow they were one entity now, nerves and capillaries fusing together to make them both stronger.

Except she had more power. She was using him, draining him. It was not a pleasant sensation. He tried to fight back, but felt something tug at his spine and thought better.

Panic tickled his skin, made his ears go hot.

"Keep calm," Glannon said, in the same tone she used to use with the horses.

A big blow came upon the shield again, and all Braig could do was brace for impact.

"Braig!" Glannon shouted. "You've got to fight with me. I can't drag your sorry carcass around! Let me do this if you won't."

He closed his eyes, reached down past the fear in his gullet, and prayed. Then he let go. He detached all that he could from his own body, closing his eyes and relaxing his muscles.

Noduuoret. Full of stars.

Down came the spinal cord arm again, sending splinters in every direction. Braig felt the repercussion all the way down his arm, making his elbow ache, feeling his own bones creak in complaint. He was going to die, right here. Curse Poole. And Glannon.

I need another arm, not more surrender.

He felt a sob well up in his throat and then heard a buzzing sound. At first he was certain it was just more of the same, the harbinger of the creature that had killed Yuri. But glancing up, Braig saw a swarm of bees flying toward him, thousands of them. They exuded a golden light and brought a sweet smell.

For a moment, he thought they were going to fight the bone creatures, but they stopped, encircling him, and then the bees alighted on his arm. In a matter of heartbeats, they began forming something at his shoulder. A cone, a long cylinder.

An arm, glowing with golden light.

She was in the eye of the storm. Aoda Kanna, daughter of a whore. Street urchin who had once had to steal pig slop just to stay alive when her mother had been abducted the first time. Fatherless. Hopeless. Friendless.

Braig had been her friend. Maybe Shenbar, too. Once.

"When I throw this in," said Poole, tying the plane clock to a long tether to his waist, "I'm going to go with it. There should be a bit of a delay—"

Beasts rose out of the roiling flesh. Reason fled. Braig was falling. Glannon was glowing. Her pupils, they exuded pure light. Every element of her being suffused with brightness unknown to mortal eyes.

Poole put his hand on Aoda's cheek.

No one had ever touched her there. The scars on her face had meant that even her mother hesitated to touch her.

"For discovery," she said softly. "For reason."

"For discovery. And home," said Poole, grabbing her hand in his and tying the turner to her wrist. "On my mark, we go."

Except as Aoda turned to thank Poole, Shenbar's pike went through his chest. So clean and perfect, bursting the buttons of the jacket that had once been the lieutenant's, traded for knowledge and help what felt like a thousand years ago. Blood sprayed on her face and into her mouth, and it tasted like iron.

Glannon Bel.

No longer, not really.

The heartbeat of the great goddess now sang in her veins, opened her mind to an infinite understanding. Braig knew it, too, she could tell. He was of her line. But he was a man. There were secrets that could only be passed from womb to womb. And Noduuoret had been waiting a long time to share them.

The gate fought her back. It had twisted her, spun out another existence beneath their feet. Great life, great death. That mystery she had taken for granted so many times, thinking that the role of a mormaer was simply to pass judgement and keep peace.

How strange, Glannon thought, to have spent so much time worrying about such a thing as the weight of a diadem on her head.

The forest creatures would come and protect them. Braig had the right idea with the bees. It was a good thing he had not surrendered himself to her completely, then. As she buffeted another blow from the maggot bear, Glannon let her consciousness flow down through her feet—where had her boots gone?—and into the flesh beneath her. Yes, she could feel the metals there. Brought across thousands of leagues, pulled from the bowels of world during the Vanishment. So impressive had that destruction been two thousand years before, it pierced and prevented the goddess from escaping, what was left of her. It warped her magic, twisted the parts that grew—the bones, the wriggling larvae—but it was meant as protection.

Come to me, thought Glannon. *Bird and bear, boar and briar. Heed the ancient call.*

Braig was quite sure one of his arms had popped out of its socket entirely while he dangled at Glannon Bel's side, doing his best to buffet the blows with the shield. He wasn't going to hold out much longer, though. Blood filled his mouth, sweat burned his eyes. And whatever she was doing to him, to move him and use him, was stealing his own life essence, such as it was.

Then relief, blessed relief. Braig turned to see the forest rising around them. Great boars, shaggy bears, and even wild horses and goats, came forth and sprang into action, shattering the bone creatures all around them. Just in time.

He understood without speaking to Glannon—she was moving his thoughts now, not long until he ceased to be anything but a man-sized object doing her will—that they needed to get closer to the center of this, where Poole was. That's where the heart of this gate was, the heart of the goddess Noduuoret.

But one glance and Braig's heart went cold, though it was bolstered by whatever force flowed from Glannon. Poole fell backward, a pike through his chest. His blood sprayed behind him, gushing with his heartbeat.

Glannon didn't need to tell him to run. As the forest itself rose to meet the force which had corrupted it for so long, they ran together toward the center of the gate.

Aoda did not think about her actions. The truth of it was as hard and as real as the ground beneath her feet. Which was not, she decided, logical. But it was real. The two things were not mutually exclusive.

"Curse you," she said to Shenbar before tackling Poole—what was left of him, bleeding and dying and crying, oh gods—and falling, falling, through the gate which welcomed them warmly like a kiss over every part of her skin, even though Shenbar was killing Wystan and there was so much sorrow, and no one knew where she'd end up because science is a question, and she was ready for an answer.

Glannon watched with the goddess's eyes as Aoda and Poole fell through the gate, the moon high above them flashing blue in an instant. There was death there, dying. But life, too. A cycle. A nothing and a something in constant battle, locked for eternity. This was just a moment, a day, a point in time.

But it was hers.

She could taste the blood of life, taste the fecundity. It was all around her.

But the gate would not close. Poole's plan was not good enough—he had planned only for his escape, but not for the healing of the Wothwood.

It cried out, wounded, still full of pain. Now, somehow, worse.

The sword. Noduuoret's. As the gate closed, she could see it lodged at the very center, bright blue, glowing as if it were moments from the forge.

"Wait," said the man.

Braig? That was his name.

"You have to let me go, Glannon. I can't let her… I have to go in after them," he said. "Aoda. She'll be alone. She'll be so alone."

Impossible. This man was hers. Claimed. Blood and body. Except…

He pleaded with her, his voice hoarse, blood coursing down his nose. She was killing him as she used him to fight, to buffet blows, to protect her holy body.

"Please, Glannon. Let me go, like you did when you thought I was dead. Let me find my name, let me find my place."

Glannon was a horror. Her hair swirled around her head, her eyes bled. Braig could feel his life being sucked dry, all his strength moving up into her body to channel the goddess.

They stood on the precipice, the gate swirling and slowly closing before them, Shenbar wrenching his glass pike from Wystan's belly, seeing Glannon—truly seeing her—and then falling to his knees. Then Caxigo up behind him, her sword to his neck, nodding, reading the signs and eyes dazzled at the sight of her goddess.

A few moments more and there would be no chance. Aoda was brilliant, but he doubted she could tend to a dying man and a new existence all together. She was his friend.

I need this redemption, he said. *For me, not for a debt. Please, Glannon. Please.*

Glannon sighed, her shoulders shuddered, and she looked down upon Braig. The animals kept the bone monsters at bay, and a strange calm fell upon all of them. She considered him, those bright eyes giving no indication of emotion or aim.

"Please," Braig begged with the last of his voice. "Please, let me go. She's got no one on the other side. Do you understand? I've got nothing here…"

For the briefest of moments, something like regret filled Glannon's features. She was not nothing, Braig knew, but this new world she was about to forge did not need him in it. Another heir to Noduuoret would make everything more confusing.

"Please, Glannon," he whispered.

"I will call you back," Glannon said then, and the whole wood spoke the words. "And you will not be able to resist the call."

For a moment, her eyes were clear again. She bent forward and looked him in the face, then leaned forward and kissed his forehead, smoothed his hair back.

"Yes," he said. The words formed a red brand on his mouth, shaping the oath. "I will heed your call."

Then she let go of his hand, peeling her fingers from his. The pain of separation was immense, pushing Braig to the edge of his already frayed stage, pulling on nerves and bone, ripping them out by the roots.

But then it was over. He was free.

"I would say to keep our people safe, but I know you will," he said to her.

And Braig fell through the gate, the oath still on his tongue, as it swallowed him whole.

From a journal entry written on the Third Day of the First Spring of the Reign of Glannon Bel, Queen of Brezhia, First Grand Mormaer.

Epilogue

WHEN GLANNON BEL, MORMAER OF THE BRIGHT BANNER CLAN, REACHED *the center of the crater known as Noduuoret's Grave, she found the goddess's great sword lodged there still.*

As she pulled the sword from its metal encasement, the world breathed a sigh of relief, the wound healed at last. The ground beneath her feet shuddered, rivulets of molten metal shooting out in every direction like a great sun. Accounts say that mines burst to life on every island, across Luthland, Theria, and the Sands. Indeed, in Brezhia it rained gold for a short time.

It is said that the creatures she had called to herself rallied around her, creating a great chain, paw and wing and warbling cry, a great entourage to Bannercliffe to destroy the Therian army awaiting them, then sweeping across the island and drowning the pirates, as well. A few survivors recalled fish leaping from the waters to devour the sailors bite by bite. But most never lived to tell the tale, though we sent plenty of birds to Yereva to let them know what to expect. Metal might have returned, but might had infused Brezhia as it had never done before. We were prepared to hold firm.

I saw Glannon return to the camp that day, two soldiers in her wake, Caxigo, Shenbar, and a throng of forest animals behind her. I saw the wood come to life again and saw in her eyes the fighting champion we had waited for in Brezhia for so long. A goddess returned.

And I believed as I have never believed before, and begged her forgiveness for harboring secrets of my own and failing to protect her as I should, for failing the memory of the goddess and planting seeds of doubt.

She did not banish me, but kept me close. Closer than anyone. And we began a new story together, and claimed the old city within, and gave it a new name: Nomina, after Glannon's earthly mother. From those ancient walls, we rebuilt and continued the story of how Brezhia rose from the ashes of war and ancient curse.